HoneyGirl

HoneyGirl

A Taste of Honey

Donna Presswood

Copyright © 2007 by Donna Presswood.
Library of Congress Control Number: 2006909891
ISBN: Hardcover   978-1-4257-4278-2
                Softcover   978-1-4257-4165-5

All rights reserved. No part of this book may be reproduced or transmitted in any form or by any means, electronic or mechanical, including photocopying, recording, or by any information storage and retrieval system, without permission in writing from the copyright owner.

This is a work of fiction. Names, characters, places and incidents either are the product of the author's imagination or are used fictitiously, and any resemblance to any actual persons, living or dead, events, or locales is entirely coincidental.

This book was printed in the United States of America.

To order additional copies of this book, contact:
Xlibris Corporation
1-888-795-4274
www.Xlibris.com
Orders@Xlibris.com

36404

My love for reading has expanded; I now have the opportunity to write for an audience. I had no idea I had this gift within me until one faithful evening when God revealed it to me.

I'm grateful to share this with others. I want to thank my children who stood for me when I thought that I would fall!

By God's favor, I think I've done it. I want to be able to say that I've done something on my own. That I have achieved the goal and also the promise that was given to me—a lifelong career of becoming an author.

Thanks! To Antoine Baker for the drawing of Honey!

I want to thank my mother and my Granddad for being the first to buy my first book!

(The Two Playful Spooks!)

I want to thank Rachael Williams from CHAC for giving me hope!

Now it is time to hold my own!

Let me introduce you to Frank and Mary William, a married black couple living in Chicago, Illinois. The two met at an early age in third grade. Frank had a major crush on Mary. The two lived in the same town not far away from one another.

Frank proposed to Mary on a beautiful Sunday night. Mary and Frank moved into their first lovely house; Mary was pregnant right off. Mary's firstborn was a boy, just what Frank wanted. Frank named his son Anthony. Frank never liked his name, so he named his son after his brother.

The couple always enjoyed each other's company, after three years, Mary was pregnant again. This time, Mary was carrying a baby girl, and oh, was she ever so happy. Mary and Frank have the love that would carry on until death does the two part. While sitting in the kitchen eating peach cobbler, Frank and Mary were reminiscing about their childhood days. Frank pours a cup of milk for Mary which she loves to drink while having her peach cobbler. The window is open, and just then a bee flew through the window. Mary jumped so high up you would have thought that she was aiming toward the ceiling.

"Dear, are you all right?" Frank asks as he smashes the bee and scoots the bee onto a piece of paper into the garbage can.

Mary put the top on the garbage can, adjusting it very tightly as if the bee were going to attack her.

"Dear, the bee is dead as it's going to get, I really killed the bee. I'm just trying to make sure that it doesn't come out of the garbage."

Mary says to Frank as she sits down at the table, "This really brings back memories, darling. I should have told you about the accident I was involved in when I was seven years of age."

She began telling Frank about the time when the family went on a trip when she was seven years old.

"I was playing with a stick while in the forest. I was pretty bored with the other children, so I distanced myself from the others and found something else to do which led to trouble. There were plenty of children around except that I was fascinated by the beehive," Mary said.

Mary was always a very busy little girl growing up, always getting herself into mischief. Mary begins to poke at the bees with the stick not knowing that she was aggravating the bees somewhat terribly. Eventually, Mary notices that the bees were not in a playful mood. That was Mary's first time playing with bees and what would be her last time ever. The bees begin attacking Mary; she tried fighting back with the stick she held in her hand, but the stick was no match for the angry bees.

Mary found herself awake inside of the hospital; she hadn't realized where she was. Mary looked around the hospital trying to gather her thoughts, and she had finally realized where she was. Mary notice her hand; she had marks all over her hand. She looks down at her legs and sees more bruises. She then begins to scream so loud that the nurse and the doctors had to come to her aid. Mary is very distraught for days to come. After this, she had to have an evaluation once a week with a psychiatrist until she was better.

Mary doesn't get better until she is almost twelve years old, and she still had nightmares about bees attacking her. Mary tells Frank that when her parents found her, she was in a fetal position; her parents thought that Mary was dead. Mary actually had stingers inside of her skin.

"My parents said that those were some strange-looking bees, they weren't any ordinary bees that attacked me that awful night. I still feel very strange myself," she says as she pours sugar inside of her milk and lots of it. Frank watches as Mary continues to pour the sugar; he grabs the sugar bowl from Mary's hand and puts the container on the table as he tells her about her sweet tooth that she has. Mary does like a lot of sweets.

Mary was eight months pregnant. All through Mary's pregnancy, she was agitated not like the pregnancy before this one. Mary sometimes goes through a great deal of pain with this pregnancy; she has no idea why. Mary amazed herself at times with the energy she has carrying this child. Little Anthony pulls his mother's blouse so as to give the baby a kiss. He lifts his mother's blouse and kisses her on the stomach. Anthony loves to feel the baby kick him. He gets a real bang out of this, this makes Anthony very excited.

Frank has realized that his wife has been a little strange throughout this pregnancy. The telephone rings; it was Mary's dad on the phone. "Hello, sweetheart, are you ready for the grand picnic?" he asks her.

"I think so," says Mary. Mary has not been to a picnic or a park since that incident as a child.

"The picnic should be a lot of fun," says her dad.

"I know," responds Mary without enthusiasm.

Frank kisses Mary and asks if she needs anything while he was going out to the store. Mary goes toward the refrigerator and sees that she's out of nectarines among other fruits. Frank says to Mary, "I know, I know," as he goes out of the door. As Frank steps out of the door, he looks at the old list he had in his pocket from the previous time he had been to the store for his wife. He says to himself, she didn't mention honey at all I should get the honey anyway. I know that Mary would be craving for honey eventually.

Frank works as a conductor. He is on his vacation, and he wants to spend every moment he could with his family. While in the bathroom the morning of the picnic, Mary is feeling a little queasy. She goes to the bathroom to take a shower. Mary's stomach begins to ball up in a tight knot; she could see the head of the baby as if the baby were coming through her skin and out of her stomach. Mary holds on to her stomach; she falls to the floor. Frank awakes to find Mary out of bed. He feels for her then he calls out her name; no response. Frank gets up and goes toward the bathroom where he finds Mary on the floor. Frank shakes his wife. When Mary comes to, she is in a deep trance as if she has no idea where she was. Frank picks Mary up from the floor, and he is surprised of what he sees on the floor oozing from between Mary's leg.

Frank lays Mary on the bed to see what the sticky substance was. He reaches for the telephone to call the hospital; at this time Mary grabs hold of Frank's arm and tells him that she's okay. Mary miraculously stands up from the bed as if nothing happened at all. She quickly goes to the bathroom and takes a shower with speed. She yells through the door and asks Frank to get breakfast ready.

Frank is amazed at his wife's quick recovery; he goes down the stairs to help prepare breakfast for the family. Mary comes down the stairs feeling very refreshed as she sits at the table and eats like she had never eaten before. Mary has eaten three nectarines, two helpings of breakfast; Mary's appetite was increasingly big. She grabs another fruit to eat. Frank looked at Mary and shook his head. He thinks to himself, that's going to be one bighead baby.

Anthony grabs his truck and begins to play with his truck as he slides his truck back and forth on the floor. Mary sits on the couch watching her son as he plays with his truck, and she hears a sound. She jumps up and begins to wave her hand as though she were waving something away from her face. Mary looks around, and there is nothing. She thinks that she heard the sound of bees. Anthony looks at his mother and asks her, "What's the matter, Mommy?" Mary looks again and there is nothing.

Mary lies back on the couch and begins to relax for a minute before it was time for the picnic. Anthony goes toward his mother and lifts up her blouse while she lies on the couch. Anthony kisses his mother. Just as he put his face down on his mom's stomach again, Anthony jumps away quickly and holds on to his face. Mary jumps up from her sleep to see her son crying and asks, "What's the matter with you, Anthony?"

Anthony points at his mother's stomach and says to her, "The baby bites me."

"Baby does not bite. Besides, the baby has to bite through me first," Mary tried to explain to Anthony. "Baby does not have any teeth yet." Mary tries to pull Anthony closer to her to give him a hug.

Anthony would not let his mother pull him any closer; he runs up the stairs into his bedroom screaming, "The baby is coming to get me," and slams his bedroom door.

Mary goes to the kitchen to sort out what she would be taking to the picnic for that afternoon. Mary thought about how Anthony reacted, she begins to laugh. Frank had come inside the house while Mary was gathering the picnic food. Anthony was upstairs playing with his play station when he had heard his dad's voice. Anthony was a good kid, Mary and Frank never had any problems with their son Anthony. Anthony couldn't wait to tell his dad about the incident with his mother's stomach.

"Dad! Dad!" yells Anthony, "you wouldn't believe what happen today. The baby bit me today while you where out!" Frank laughs at Anthony as he lifts him from the floor.

Mary says to Frank, "Your kid with the big imagination."

"No! Mom, it really happened, the baby bit me," says Anthony. Anthony was so loud you would have thought the next-door neighbors had heard him.

"What is he talking about? Asks Frank.

"I have no idea," says Mary. Anthony grabs a fruit off the table as he runs upstairs to finish playing.

"I think we had better start getting prepared for the barbecue picnic," says Frank to his wife.

"I guess we had better," says Mary.

"Are you sure you are up to this?" asks Frank.

"Yes, I'm very sure," Mary assures her husband.

Mary is having mild contraction, which is nothing to worry about; she knows that this is not her time just yet. While putting bags into the truck, Mary decides to take a seat inside of the truck. Frank is just about done putting everything inside the truck, when Anthony comes down the stairs. "Oops! I almost forgot about you, good thing you come from out of the bedroom."

Frank carried Anthony to the truck, and says to Mary, "Look who we almost forgot." Frank points to Anthony. "We have loaded up everything but our son." Mary and Frank start to laugh. The baby begins to move about inside of Mary's stomach as she laughs.

Mary held her stomach; she tells Frank that "This baby is too hyperactive, dear." "This baby feels like she's jumping on a trampoline or something." Frank laughs at Mary's remark. There is silence for a quick second; a cry was heard, and Mary's eyes got real big.

Frank asks Mary, "Is there a baby doll or some sort of toy inside of the truck? I could have sworn that I've heard a baby cry."

"I heard it also," says Mary, "and it was loud and clear."

"I heard the baby cry too," says Anthony, "just like that baby bit me too."

The three sit quietly for a brief two minutes. The sound of the baby crying was no more. Mary is now eight centimeters and has no idea at all. The family has arrived to the picnic; everyone is there at the picnic. Frank has helped with taking the food out of the truck while Mary sits still inside of the truck. Mary is sort of hesitant, remembering that this is the same forest she recalled as a child.

"Of the entire place in the world to be, why this same place?" Mary says to herself. Mary didn't like this, not one bit.

Frank was done gathering things from the truck. He tells Mary, "I have one more big load, and that's you. What's taking you so long to get out of the truck?"

Mary tells Frank that "This is the forest I was telling you about when I was a little girl. I just never knew of the name, but I'll never forget this place as long as I live."

"I'm going to protect you, my dear, I would not let anything happen to you," Frank says to his wife.

Mary decides to get out of the truck and mingle with the crowd. She sits down with her parents at the table. "I didn't have any idea we were coming to this place," says Mary's dad. "If I had known, I wouldn't have come."

"Yes, dear, we found out this morning when we ask for directions, and it was too late to turn around," Mary's mom assures her.

"Just try and enjoy yourself," says Mary's dad.

"I will try," says Mary as she grabs a piece of ribs from the pot and nibbles on the piece, taking a bottle of honey from her bag. She pours some on her ribs to get a good taste from the meat.

Chancy tells Mary, "You are something else with that honey."

Mary says to her mother, "If you don't have one without the other, it's not good."

"If you say so, dear," Chancy replied. Mary sat openly eating her food as she licks her fingers. The bees are buzzing while Mary's baby within her is moving about in such a force that you would think that the baby was about to jump out of Mary's stomach. Mary does not like this feeling. She is afraid; she runs to the truck, jumps inside of the truck, and locks the doors and rolls up the windows. Mary had felt threatened by the sound of the bees buzzing as though the bees were getting very close to her, so Mary ran out of fear. While inside of the truck, Mary's mother comes to check on her. She asks if she is okay.

"I was trying to get away from the bees, Mom," says Mary.

"What bees, dear? I didn't see any bees at all," says Chancy.

"You mean to tell me you didn't hear anything," asks Mary.

"No! Dear, I have not seen or heard anything," says Chancy.

"You are going deaf, Mother dear," says Mary.

"Well, when you come out from the truck, I'll still be out by the grill barbecuing," says Chancy.

Mary's about to take a sip from her can of pop until she is interrupted by her husband. Little does Mary know that there is a bee on the can of her pop. Mary let the window down so that she could speak to Frank for a brief minute.

"Why you are inside of the truck?" Frank asks Mary.

"I feel a lot comfortable here," says Mary, "I'll come out in a few."

"Okay, dear, if you need me, I'm playing ball with the guys, okay," says Frank.

"Okay," Mary responds.

Mary put the can of pop to her lip and sips from the can; the bee is trying to communicate with Mary although she had no idea. Mary moves about too fast as she opens her mouth to scream, but the bee flew right into Mary's mouth, she swallows the bee. You could see the movement inside of Mary's stomach. She tries very hard to cough up the bee.

Mary is going through a mass of things at that quick moment; she really doesn't have any idea what she should do. Mary decides to open the truck door to climb out. Mary rolls to the ground and is having hard pains inside of her. Mary was experiencing sharp pains, which don't feel like contractions at this moment. It feels like an electric shock as well as stinging. Mary's body is shaking as though a fight was taking place inside of her body and she couldn't do anything about it. Mary has no idea what is going on inside of her. The bee is merely protecting her. But Mary has no idea she's about to fall apart.

Frank runs to Mary's aid, and so does everyone else. Mary is helped from the ground. As Mary is getting up from the ground, the bee shoots up and out of Mary's mouth like a bolt of lightning. Mary gags as she spits and wipes her mouth. Frank quickly stomped on the bee and grabs Mary and puts her inside of the truck. Frank drives his wife to a nearby hospital, Mary is quickly seen by a doctor.

Mary explains the whole ordeal to the doctor, and he doesn't believe anything Mary has said to him. Frank wouldn't have believed anything either, if he hadn't seen the bee fly from Mary's mouth. Frank tells Mary, "All you need is some rest, and I'm going to make sure you get some rest."

The doctor has Mary under observation for that night; he has assured Mary that the baby would not be born for a couple of weeks even though she was eight centimeters. Mary said to herself, that's what the doctor thinks. This baby would definitely be born tonight.

Mary tells Frank that she is hungry and she wants something to eat, such as something very sweet. Frank knows what time this is. Frank goes to get his wife what she craves for, this makes Mary happy, and she is content for the night. That same night, Mary feels very moist between the legs: she is very uncomfortable. Mary's body is going through a dramatic turn at that moment. She wants to scream; then she wants to laugh; she is going through moods that shock her body. Mary tries not to wake Frank up. Frank was asleep on the chair next to Mary's bed. Mary's eyes begin to roll in the back of her head as she goes into a deep trance. Mary has to close her eyes at this moment; when Mary opens her eyes, there between her legs was her newborn baby.

Mary's eyes open very wide at this extraordinary event that just took place right in her face. Mary got up and went to the bathroom to clean the baby. She is too amazed at the strength she had within her. Mary later returns to her bed to be with her baby girl. Mary decides to wake Frank to tell him that the baby was born. Frank was happy to see that the baby was born, and she says to Frank, "The doctor does not know that the baby was born just yet."

Frank looks at his wife with astonishment. "What are you talking about?" asks Frank.

"The baby came out on her own with no help from the doctor; she just slid right out of me," says Mary.

Frank continues to stare at Mary with a look of dismay. She has to call out to Frank twice to get his attention. Just then a doctor walked inside of the room and sees Mary holding a baby.

The doctor asks Mary, "Did another doctor deliver the baby without my knowledge?"

"No one delivered my baby. She decided to come out on her own without help."

"You've got to be jiving me," says the doctor to Mary.

"No, I kid you not," says Mary to the doctor.

The doctor calls for another doctor and nurse to come inside to examine the baby to see if everything is okay. Later that evening, the baby was brought to Mary's room by the same doctor. Frank was a very proud father that day.

Mary says to Frank, "This pregnancy was very much different from the last one. I was more energetic with this baby girl than I were with the baby boy." Mary holds her baby real tight toward her breast, and she says to Frank, "This baby has the strangest eyes. I thought that a newborn baby's eyes don't open until a couple days."

"That is strange," says Frank. "Well, with this new breed of generation, you would never know what's new. Next thing you know these newborn baby would come out of the womb walking. You'll never know what's next. This little girl does have the strangest eyes. It's like she's checking me out in the weirdest way."

"The baby's eyes are a deep dark color and she's gorgeous as ever," says the doctor as he walks inside the room. "The baby did the strangest thing earlier when we were examining her. She made the funniest sound; it sounded like a buzzing sound, and we all had to look at one another." Frank and Mary smile at each other as if to say to the doctor, if you only knew what we're going through.

Mary and Frank left the hospital to take their newborn baby home. Once home Mary and Frank were greeted by their parents. Chancy had stayed at Mary's house so as to take care of Anthony. As soon as Chancy notices her grandchild, she says to Mary. "Why, her eyes are so dark."

"I think her eyes are so gorgeous," says Mary.

"I think they're mystical, that's what her eyes look like to me," says Chancy.

Mary asks Anthony to take a look at his little sister. Anthony walks over took a quick peek stood back as far as he could. Frank asks, "Anthony, what seems to be the problem, son. Don't you like your new sister?"

"Yes! I just don't want to be to close to her, last time she bit me," says Anthony.

Chancy starts to laugh at her grandson. "What are you talking about?" asks Chancy.

"I don't want to touch the baby because last time the baby bit me while inside of Mommy's stomach."

"The baby did what?" Chancy laughs out loud. "You are something else, what would you think of next?" says Chancy.

Mary and Frank haven't said a word. One day while Frank was at work, Mary was in the room feeding her baby. Mary also tries to feed herself; this is getting very uncomfortable for her and also the baby. Mary props the baby bottle on her chest while trying to eat from her plate. "Honey, can Mommy take a couple of more spoons, and I'll be right with you," she says to her baby which she calls Honey.

Frank calls her his Honey girl. Honey keeps Mary and Frank up half of the night. The only chance Mary has the time to eat was when Honey's asleep or when Frank is home from work to help out with Honey. Honey is a very frisky baby; and when she couldn't have her way, she would have a tantrum. Frank has Honey girl attached to him. He had always wanted a baby girl. Although he has his son, he is so attached to his daughter.

Mary reaches for a bite to eat, and by this time Honey is agitated; she begins to cry and kick at the same time. Only because Mary starts to feed her face even more. Honey looks at her mother as her eyes start to go around in circles. Mary stopped eating to feed the baby at once; she was very startled at this. What is going on here, asks Mary to herself.

Later that evening, Mary tells Frank about what had happened with her and Honey that morning. "What is really going on here?" asks Frank, "do you think that we should go get Honey girl checked out?"

"No," said Mary, "Those people will not be using my child as a guinea pig."

Frank kisses his baby on the forehead and calls her his Honey girl, and she smiles at him while she coos. Every day, there was always something unusual with Honey girl. Honey is now seven months old, and she's gotten to be as beautiful as she grows older.

Mary is eating her nectarine while Honey is sitting in her lap seat. Honey reaches out toward Mary's nectarine indicating that she would like some of Mary's nectarine. Mary, knowing that her child has no tooth in her mouth, couldn't possibly give her any. Honey is upset by this; she begins another of her tantrums. This time, Mary hears the sound of buzzing but very lightly. She starts to look around the room. Then at Honey. Now this is impossible, says Mary to herself. Mary explains this to her husband. Frank tells Mary to keep this between the two of them and no one else. Other people wouldn't understand this situation because right now they cannot understand.

"No need for others to get involved, it would only complicate things even more," says Frank.

Time has gone by; Honey girl is now the age of three, and she's very advance for her age. Honey girl and Anthony are in the bedroom playing together; while Mary was cleaning up around the house. Anthony is now six years old now. Some days the two would get along with one another, and some days the two would not; this happens to be one of those days. Mary knew that the two always aggravated each other as children tend to do.

Honey girl and Anthony are playing on the floor with the toys. Honey girl reaches over to grab Anthony's truck, and Anthony grabs his truck away from Honey girl. Honey girl grabs the truck away from Anthony and stung him very lightly. Anthony yells out real loud; Mary comes out of the room to see what was happening. When Mary arrives to the bedroom, Honey girl had her brother against the wall.

"What is going on here?" The two point to each other to say that the other had started it. "I don't know which one of you started this, but I'm about to end this right now," says Mary.

"Mom, you need to put her back where she came from" says Anthony.

"Well, I think Honey is a little too big to go back inside of me," says Mary to Anthony.

"You should have put her back when I first told you," says Anthony.

Anthony has been through it all with his sister; sometimes he wouldn't tell his Mom being afraid of his sister at times. Anthony would just sit in the middle of the floor and say to himself, Honey is a bad, bad, bad girl. Anthony just shakes his head at first. "She took my cookie just the other day; now she's getting away with taking my truck. What's next?" asks Anthony, Honey girl frowns at her brother as she plays with her doll.

Anthony does not bother with his sister very much. He has learned to stay out of her way. Anthony knows just when to be with his sister.

Mary and Frank take the children to the kid's stop, a place where the children could have more fun then fun. They have pizza and soda pops; after the children are done eating, they go into the game room to play games. The children decides to play inside of the ball pin. They start to throw the balls with full force. Anthony does not like this. One ball hits him in the face. Honey does not like this at all; she had to get involved. Her brother was hit with a ball. Honey has noticed that half of the children were much older than her and her brother. Although Honey was only three going on thirty, you wouldn't have known this unless you're around her to know her.

Honey grabs Anthony to help him out of the site; Anthony tries throwing plastic balls. Honey girl tells Anthony to "come on, we don't need to be inside of this place. The children were acting very rudely."

Honey's eyes start to go around in circles, and her eyes are getting bigger as she gets agitated. Anthony starts to watch Honey girl's finger; Anthony knows the feel from that one finger. He had been touched by that one finger quite often.

The little boy who was throwing the balls very wildly at the other children hasn't noticed that he was being targeted by Honey. Honey girl touches the boy lightly and the little boy screams out. This gave attention to the parent; Honey has eased her way from the plastic ball pen. She and Anthony go to play another game; the boy is crying too much to notice that Honey has gotten away to play somewhere else.

One boy has seen Honey girl's eyes, and he was still petrified. He has not moved from his spot; but he is pointing in Honey's direction trying to get a word out from his mouth. When the parent asks what happened, the others trample over one another trying to get out from the plastic ball pen. The children did not want to play anymore that day, which was very strange to some of the parents. "I think you had enough excitement for the day," one of the parents says to her son. He wouldn't respond to his mother at all; he kept looking at her in her face.

While at home that night, Mary asked Honey if she had anything to do? With that commotion back at the Kid's spot that evening.

"I don't recall," says Honey to her mother. Anthony starts to laugh at his sister.

Frank says to Honey girl as he shook his head, "What am I to do with you."

Honey girl grabs her dad around his leg and says to him, "You are going to tell me that you love me and all is well."

"I love you," says Frank to his daughter.

Time goes by and Honey has grown to be even more beautiful than ever. Honey's eyes are the most amazing, the first thing a male would notice of her besides her body. Honey has grown up to be a very busy bee. As Honey grows up, she has noticed a lot about her significant body. No one else knows about Honey's ordeal except the immediate family, not even the grandparents. Mary doesn't know how her parents would react to the situation.

Honey is now at the age of sixteen; she's on the track team and she's a speedy runner. Honey's social life is not overcoming. She does little of this only because she feels awkward toward the others, meaning that if the other teenager had any idea of her strange behavior, they would think that she was a freak; Honey really keeps a low profile. Honey is on the track team for merely a week; the original track teacher is off for a week. The new coach wanted to start the team off by letting the team race one on one just to break the team in.

Coach Bob says to the team, "I need a boy and a girl right now!" He points out Honey and Gerald.

The team of boys begins to laugh, even Gerald, as he says to Honey, "I'll give you a head start," trying to be very funny. Honey did not find this to be a bit funny at all. She steps away to get into her running mode. Coach Bob says his get-ready speech; he's just about to say go, and both of the runners shot out just when he said the word *go*. Gerald was in the lead for a quick second while his guys cheer him on. Honey speeds past him with no sweat off her back as she gains up on him and leaves Gerald behind. Coach Bob couldn't believe his eyes.

He says to the two, "My ticking clock must not be tocking right, as of now I know that was the fastest race I've seen says coach Bob!" The coach signals for the two to run the race again. "Go!" And the two shoot off with speed as Honey leaves Gerald behind again. Coach Bob is ever so excited, he says to Honey, "You have got to be the fastest runner in the century, I might add." Gerald felt like a dried-up duck; he was laid out on the ground gasping for breath while Honey stood without a sweat from her eyebrow or body.

The team looks at Honey with amazement. Honey could have run faster than that. She keeps the running to a level. Honey doesn't realize that excitement brings out a lot hidden inside of Honey. Coach Bob decides to let the whole team race to the end of the school block and back. Meaning to go around the whole school and back. He drops his hand down and signals for the team to go. Just as the coach says, "Go!" Honey was at the coach's side. "What are you waiting for? I said for you all to go, didn't you hear me?"

Honey shook her head at the coach and says to him, "I went!"

He begins to scratch the top of his head as Honey walked away. Honey is getting agitated; she wants to end the day quickly; she was not feeling the day. She wanted to quickly let this day go past as quick as it came by, so she thought that if she could speed up with her running, everything would go as fast as she expected it to.

Coach Bob tells the class, "Let's do this one more time, thanks to smarty-pants with the almighty wings on. The class was very frustrated and a little upset with Honey for the second laps that they would have to do because of her.

"I got my eye on you," says Coach Bob.

At that moment a car pulls up and out stepped an attractive parent, Coach Bob turn't his head for a quick second, that was all Honey needed. Honey puts on full speed and quickly bypassed the class with the quickness. While doing so, the class is dodging and waving as the team is running from the noise that the team is hearing in the air. Two of the guys look up, and one of the guys asks the other, "Do you hear the sound of bees?"

"Yes," says the other guy, and the two took off very fast as they try and run for shelter. Most of the team are swinging as they run for shelter.

While running, Honey felt her back feeling very funny although she ignores the situation and keeps on running full speed ahead. Honey is the last to take off and the first to make it back, standing right in the coach's face. The rest of the team are wheezing and trying to make it to the coach as fast as they could. Honey never loses her breathe, not once. Some were pulling out asthma pumps and sharing their asthma pump with the others as they tried to move.

"Did you see her move?" the coach asks the attractive lady who stood next to him.

The woman pauses. "I've seen her standing right next to you," she says to Coach Bob.

"No! Did you see her run with the crowd? Says Coach Bob. "I was watching you."

"Watching me?" says the woman. "I have no idea."

"This is not over with. This is not the last you've heard from me," says Coach Bob while looking dumbfounded.

"Yeah, whatever, Psycho Bob," Honey mumbles. Honey walks toward the shower so that she could freshen up. While inside of the shower, Honey receives a tap on the shoulder; she was startled at that moment. Honey quickly turns around, and to her surprise, there was a young girl standing outside of her shower. The young girl introduces herself as Eliza than Honey introduces herself while Honey tried to cover herself up quick.

"How did you get those strange holes into your back?" asks Eliza. "They look like a couple of deep marks."

"I do not recall having any marks on my back," Honey says to Eliza.

"Well! Duh. I'm not blind I see what I see," says Eliza to Honey.

Honey has no idea what was really going on, and she just met Eliza. "Could I believe someone I've just met?" Honey walks toward the mirror to take a look at her back, and to her surprise she could see the marks on her back. The two watched in the mirror as the marks disappear.

Honey asks Eliza to never say anything about this to anyone. "I would not tell anyone" says Eliza, "as long as you'll be my friend."

Honey goes to put on her clothes, and Eliza is standing. Honey turns away to have some privacy. Honey says to herself, this is getting to be too weird for me; I don't know what is going on with my body. What if I weren't wearing a blouse? I would have sprouted out some wings or something and everyone would have thought of me as being a crazy girl.

Quickly, Honey and Eliza became the best of friends; they are somewhat alike. The only difference is that Eliza is an only child and Honey is not. Honey is a loner by choice, not by force. While on the other hand, Eliza's case is different. Eliza was a loner by force and not by choice. Honey enjoys being with Eliza; not one day goes by when those two aren't together. They only grew closer and closer to one another as the days and weeks went by. Honey felt something totally special about Eliza, that there was some goodness inside of Eliza. Or is it that Eliza wouldn't let up? Or is it that Eliza knows something about Honey which no one else does, and Honey is afraid that Eliza would spill some beans out of the bag?

No! Honey really enjoys Eliza's company, and the two have come to trust one another over the weeks. The two walk home together mostly every day talking to one another has done the both justice. The two stayed on the telephone together talking a lot.

The two were together at the park sitting on the bench talking when Jim walks up. Jim introduces himself to the girls as he reaches out his hand to shake hands. Eliza shook hands with Jim. Although Honey was skeptical, she shook hands with Jim. "I notice you two at school," says Jim. The two were quiet for a brief minute with nothing to say.

Honey decides to speak out first, "Do you live close by?" asks Honey.

"Yes, I live around the corner from you," says Jim.

"How close for me not to notice you," says Honey to Jim.

"Well, I can't help but to notice you," says Jim.

"I was wondering if I could take you out if I'm not being to blunt," says Jim. "There is no sense in prolonging sitting here if I'm going to get shot down. So I might as well say what I'm going to say and get it over with."

"I don't do the out thing," says Honey. Eliza nudges Honey slightly.

"I'll think about it," says Honey. Jim went inside of his pocket and pulled out a piece of paper and hands the paper to Honey. Eliza reaches out and grabbed the piece of paper before Honey could.

"I'll make sure Honey calls you," says Eliza to Jim.

Jim walked away from the two girls. Honey and Eliza giggle as Jim walks away and look back at the two.

"Are you going to go out with Jim?" asks Eliza.

"I don't know," says Honey, "I've never been out with a guy before. My parents would kill me."

"He'll probably take you to the movies," says Eliza.

"Or out to eat dinner or something," says Honey.

"Jim is very cute," says Eliza. "I wonder, does he have a brother?"

"When I call him tonight, I'll ask that question," says Honey, "and maybe we could double-date and I'll feel comfortable." Honey and Eliza walk home the shortcut way. Honey has to pass Eliza's house before she would get to her house. The two decide to race and as usual, Honey gives Eliza a head start then passes her up once the two reach their destiny.

Eliza goes inside of her house; she waves to Honey telling her that she would call her as soon as she thinks Honey made it inside of the house. Just as Honey walks inside of the house, the telephone rings, and Anthony picks up the telephone. "Guess who?" says Anthony. Honey grabs the telephone from Anthony and tells him to leave Eliza alone.

The two talk on the telephone for fifteen minutes before Mary walks inside of the house. "Who's on the telephone?" asks Mary. Anthony hears his mother come in from work; he gives her a kiss.

"I'm talking to Eliza!" Honey tells her mother.

"Mom, now you know that's the only person who calls here for Honey!"

"Well, you never know one day Honey would get other calls from someone," says Mary.

"Yes, I guess she would," says Anthony.

"Is that your brother I hear in the background?" asks Eliza.

"Yes, that's my bighead brother you hear!"

"Mom, you know that Eliza is Honey's second shadow, she's around more than Honey's own shadow." The other line buzzes, and Honey asks Eliza to hold on while she gets the other line.

"Hello?" asks Honey.

"Hello to you!" says the person on the other line.

"Who is this?" asks Honey.

"This is Jim."

"How did you get my telephone number?" asks Honey.

"I have my ways," says Jim.

"Hold on for a minute," says Honey to Jim.

"It's him!" says Honey to Eliza."
"Him who?" asks Eliza.
"Jim, the guy from the park," says Honey.
"I'll call you back," says Honey.
"Don't forget," says Eliza. Anthony notices that Honey's done, went into her bedroom with the telephone.
"I'm watching you," Anthony yells to Honey.
Frank walks inside of the house and says, "Honey, I'm home." Mary gives her husband a kiss and asks what he wants for dinner.
"We're going out for dinner if my family does not mind," says Frank. "Where is my other Honey?"
"Oh, she's on the telephone talking in private, and I don't think it's Eliza," says Anthony. Honey comes from the bedroom and gives her Dad a kiss on the cheek.
"How about going out to eat tonight?" asks Frank.
"That's fine with me," says Honey.
The family leaves to go out to eat that night. The family really enjoys the beautiful night at the restaurant. While sitting at the restaurant, Anthony tells Honey that he has a secret.
Honey asks, "And what is that, dear nosy brother of mines?"
"I know this guy who likes you, and he wants to take you out," says Anthony.
"Who might that be?" asks Honey.
"I think you already know who that person is," says Anthony.
"Maybe I do or maybe I don't," says Honey.
"Don't kid me!" says Anthony. "That's the reason you went into your bedroom to talk privately, I know you by now."
"If you say anything to Mom and Dad, I'll let you have it so bad you would never get over what I'll do to you," says Honey.
"Okay," says Anthony, "I'm not going to say anything. Jim is a cool guy; I like him. He's been asking about you."
"So you gave him our telephone number?" asks Honey.
"No, I didn't give our number out," says Anthony.
"I wonder how he got our telephone number," says Honey.
"There are all sorts of ways a person could get your telephone number," says Anthony.
"Yes, especially if they're interested in you," says Mary. The two are shocked to know that their mother is listening in their conversation.
"So you have a friend?" asks Frank.

"Just someone I've met at the park," says Honey, "nothing special!"
"Obviously he thinks that you're special," says Anthony.
"So are you going to go out with him?" asks Mary.
"I don't know, I'm not into boys just yet."
"Don't trust any guy," says Frank.
"Make sure you have your guards up every moment," says Mary.
"I aware of that," says Honey.

The family had their quality time together that evening while enjoying dinner. As soon as Honey returns home, she couldn't wait to get on the telephone to call Eliza with the good news about her telling her parents.

The next evening while on her date with Jim, Honey hardly said a word unless Jim said something to her.

Honey tells Jim to excuse her behavior. "It's just that I've never been on a date before."

"Don't worry," says Jim, "I'm not going to bite you." He jokes with her." The two are at the movie, and Jim tries to put his arms around Honey. And to her defense, she stings him unexpectedly when he touches her body.

"I'm sorry," Honey says to Jim.
"I guess I have some electricity in my body," says Honey.
"Ouch! And a whole lot of it" says Jim, "I must say!"

Jim keeps his arm close to his side without moving them again that night while at the movies. The two leave and have dinner at a fine restaurant. Honey starts to open up as the night comes. The two decide to take a walk in the park to stretch out a little.

While in the park, they see that there are others enjoying the fresh air that night? Honey couldn't believe that she is enjoying herself that night; she couldn't wait to tell Eliza about her first date with Jim. The two would have a lot more to talk about when Honey tells Eliza about her night out with Jim. Honey starts to loosen up just a little bit more; Jim didn't know if he should touch Honey again or just wait for her advances. He says to himself, if I wait for her advances, I'll never get a good-night kiss.

This time Jim did the smart thing, he thought about asking Honey first before approaching her. Honey tells him not on the first night.

"I can understand," says Jim. "I hope I see you again."

"You will," she tells Jim. "I really enjoyed myself," she adds as the two prepare for Jim to take Honey home from their date.

Honey arrives home and the family is up and waiting on her. Honey comes inside of the house with her keys, and she hears noises. When she opens the door and steps inside, there is no one there. Honey is surprised to see no one's up. The time is ten-thirty at night. And her family is always up this time of the night, especially on the weekend. Honey knocks on her parents' bedroom door. Frank comes to the door pretending he's been asleep. Honey asks where is mom. Mary comes from underneath the covers pretending to be asleep.

Honey says to her parents, "I know you all weren't asleep this early on a weekend." Frank starts to laugh.

"Why did you give us away?" says Mary, "now she's going to think that we are spying on her."

"I knew you two weren't asleep this early," says Honey as she goes to her bedroom. Anthony comes home from work and asks Honey how her date with Jim was.

"Oh, it went real well," says Honey.

"It better go real well or I would have to hurt somebody," says Anthony.

The following weeks have come and gone by, and Honey feels closer to Jim. Honey and Eliza sit at the table eating fruits. Honey has gotten Eliza in the habit of eating plenty of nectarines.

Eliza asks Honey, "Have you asked Jim if he has a brother as I've asked you?"

"You know what, Eliza? Jim is an only child such as you," says Honey.

"Oh!" says Eliza as she held her face in her hand. "Now isn't that something."

"Well! Does he have a friend, a distant cousin somewhere out there?" says Eliza. She is now about to sound very desperate. "Look, it looks like I'm losing you to him. I can't deal with this. You're my best friend. In fact, the only friend I've got in the whole world."

"I tell you what I'll ask, does he have a friend or a longtime uncle out there somewhere?" says Honey.

"I didn't say uncle!" says Eliza.

"Well! That would have come next," says Honey. "Why not run through the whole family."

"Don't be funny," says Eliza to Honey. The two start to laugh at each other.

"How about the two of us having a slumber party while my parents take their weekend vacation?" says Honey?

"When this would be?" asks Eliza.

"This weekend," says Honey.

"Cool! Who would we invite?" says Eliza.

"I don't know right off but we'll find someone," says Honey.

The next week Honey goes out with Jim; this night Honey thought to herself, maybe tonight I'll do something different, I'll let him kiss me. After all it's been a couple weeks we've been going out. While the two are at the park standing by a tree, it starts to get a little chilly out. Jim, being polite, takes off his jacket and covers Honey. Honey feels like she's Jim's girl although Jim has told everyone in school that Honey is his girl. Jim asks Honey for a kiss, and to his surprise, she told him yes.

The two kiss, and Honey likes it. Honey pulls Jim closer to her and begins to lock lips with him. Jim likes every minute of this, and so does Honey. The two tongues are really so locked you couldn't pry them apart with some lock cutters. Honey has never felt the way she is feeling that night. She feels very loose as her body starts to heat up. Honey starts to unfasten her blouse; she doesn't know what's come over her as she feels the heat vibrating from within her.

Jim is getting very excited as he realizes that Honey about to take it all off. Honey eyes begin to roll in the back of her head as she pulls Jim more closely to her. The two falls to the grass, feeling nothing but passion; the two do not realize they had fallen. They are too sexually aroused to notice. Honey is at the bottom while Jim lies on top of her to finish opening her blouse.

Honey does not know why her body is going through the changes and if this the way she is supposed to feel. Jim continues; he begins to kiss Honey on her breast and on her lips, enjoying every taste of honey-sweet juices that are coming from her mouth. The more the two kiss, the more juices come from her mouth, getting thicker and tasting even sweeter.

Honey decides to roll over on Jim at this moment. She is feeling intimidated by Jim being on the top; Honey starts to lick Jim's lip as if she were sampling his lips before swallowing him whole. The more the two kiss, the more juices are replenished from her mouth. Honey has a tight grip on Jim's head. Jim starts to pull away from Honey's grip as she held him closer to her mouth. Honey's body begins to experience some changes at this moment as she goes into a deep trance. Honey decides to let go of Jim's head as she lays his head gently on the grass.

Jim looks Honey in her eyes, and the only thing Jim could see is blackness. Jim is very frightened at this moment to see Honey like this. He tries to get up, but Honey wouldn't let Jim move. She held him with every strength that she had. She looks down at Jim as he lies there on the grass helpless. She then pukes out the juices into Jim's face which she had accumulated while the two had kissed so passionately. Jim lies there without knowing what to do, he has no idea what had just taken place. He crawls from underneath Honey and runs as fast as he could while wiping his face.

Honey walks through the park with no idea of what took place with her body or mind. Honey is in a state in which her body has control of her every thought of concentration. Honey has never experienced the touch of a man before; her body has been through a dramatic sensation in which she has no control over. Honey does not realize that she would not ever be able to enjoy sex with a man except only to become sexually aroused by a man's touch. Honey's body can't take too much, only to discover that she's half-and-half. Honey has the power of a queen bee.

Honey's body begins to manifest as she walks around the park in a deep trance. Honey's body goes through a tremendous state of shock as she starts to release secretion of honey from the pores of her body. As you hear the sound of Honey buzzing, Honey stands in the wild darkness as the bees are summoned to her body. Honey stands as she attracts all bees toward her; she was covered from head to toe as she stood still in the park.

Nature has taken its course, and Honey has no idea until the manifestation is complete. Honey would soon come to realize why she felt different from others more than she had realized. Honey comes out from the trance to realize that she's half-naked and could not remember much. Honey runs home which was not too far from the park; she opens the back door, sneaks inside, and takes her a quick shower.

That night while in bed, Honey cries to herself not really knowing what had come over her that night. Honey looks at the moon while lying in her bed trying to think. As she starts to think, everything comes to her slowly. Honey didn't know what to believe "was I dreaming" Honey asked herself. Honey decides to give Jim a call just to see how far she was with what was actually going on. Maybe Jim could explain what happened to her and why he had left her wandering in the park all alone. Honey picks up the telephone to call Jim. As soon as he hears Honey's voice, he quickly hangs up the phone. Honey had actually heard the click loud and clear.

"Ouch! Damn what I did," says Honey.

Honey lies in her bed watching outside of her window, and she sees a bee outside of the window trying to get inside of her bedroom. Honey opens the window without really knowing why. The bee flew around Honey and landed on her shoulder. Everything comes back to Honey as if it were a dream. She remembers the bees surrounding her body to protect her from all things. Honey now realized what colony that's within her. The bees are not there to harm her. They're there to comfort and to protect her also. The bee that Honey let inside was called the queen bee. She's there to protect Honey.

"I really feel that I'm dreaming," says Honey as she watches the bee sit calmly on her shoulder. Honey falls asleep as she's very exhausted from what took place tonight.

That morning, Honey wakes up with the smell of breakfast cooking. Honey goes inside of the kitchen feeling very famished. She sat at the table.

"How was your night last night?" asks Frank while he puts in front of Honey a plate of bacon, eggs, and pancakes with lots of honey just like she likes it.

"You were very tired last night; your mother tried waking you last night, but you wouldn't bulge. We figure you have to be awfully tired so we let you be. So how are you feeling?" asks Frank.

"I'm feeling very drain," says Honey.

"Why that is?" Frank asks Honey.

"Something happened to me last night, Dad, it was the strangest thing ever," says Honey.

"I had never kissed anyone before nor have I had sex before," she tells her dad. "This particular night I really wanted to, although I didn't."

"Shouldn't you be talking to your mother about this?" says Frank. "I don't know anything about the birds and the bees."

"Strange you should use those words," says Honey. "That's what I would like to talk to you about as well as talk to Mom."

"Well, let me wake your mother up right now. I think she has slept long enough." Frank scurries to wake Mary.

"I think your daughter is ready to talk to you," Frank tells Mary.

"Why can't she talk to you, Frank, I'm still trying to get some sleep," says Mary.

"It's about the birds and the bees," says Frank to Mary.

"Oh! Then I've better get up from here. I'm on my way," says Mary.

Mary arrives to the kitchen within five minutes no sooner.

"What's wrong, dear?" she asks as she sat down at the table to eat breakfast.

"I feel like a freak," says Honey to her parents.

"Why do you say that?" asks Mary.

"I had my first kiss and I went about it the wrong way," says Honey.

"Why do you say that?" asks Frank.

"First tell me that you didn't give up the goodies," says Mary as she sat down at the table. Frank taps Mary on the hand to silence her.

"No, Mom". I don't think that I could have gone that far. Something held me back.

"What do you mean?" asks Frank as he held his bacon between his teeth. Mary was very quiet as she waits to hear Honey's answer.

"I puked up all over Jim's face," says Honey, "as we kissed". Frank's bacon flew out of his mouth as he tries to take in what Honey just said.

"Honey, why would you puke up on someone?" Frank asks.

"I ask myself that question," says Honey.

"Was it something you ate? Asks Mary.

"Definitely not," says Honey.

"I was getting very full just by getting arouse. I don't think I should be talking to my parents about this stupid subject," says Honey.

"No, Honey, as long as you didn't have sex with this guy. You didn't?" asks Mary.

"No, Mom and Dad, I did not do the do," says Honey.

"That's good to know!" says Frank.

"I want to know why I feel the way I feel when I'm sexually excited," asks Honey.

"How do you feel, Honey?" asks Mary.

"I feel like I want to devour my prey at that moment," says Honey.

"Your prey?" asks Mary.

"Yes, this is what the person feels like once they're in my clutches at that moment," explains Honey. "Then I start to get full then I puke on him after I've gotten what I wanted from him. He was so helpless, I felt as though he were a prey of some sort."

"That's very odd!" says Frank to Honey.

"I'm just not into males that way, Mom and Dad; I swear that Jim looks like a steak to me at that moment. If I hadn't felt full, I would have eaten him alive," says Honey. "The best thing that happened was the way I felt at that moment; strange thing is at the moment of being aroused, I had no feeling toward him. He was just meat. I had to actually maintain my composure, so that was one of the reasons I had to puke on Jim. I felt bad later when I thought about what I'd done to him. I know he'll never go out with me again ever in life."

"Don't worry about that," says Frank, "it would all come to an end. I guess we should tell you about your situation."

Mary and Frank decide to tell Honey about Mary's past. Honey sits through the whole conversation without a word, just all ears. Honey couldn't believe her ears although she had no choice but to believe her parents.

"Also what took place just the other night?"

Anthony walks inside the house, kisses his mom on the cheek, and grabs a seat.

"What's with the sad face?" asks Anthony.

"We spoke with your sister about her situation," says Frank.

Good! Said Anthony.

The next day at school Honey was very distant from Eliza as if she wanted no part of her. Honey has no idea that there were more to her strange behavior than what she had already felt.

"Now I'm a freak and a stupid insect," says Honey to herself.

Now what else would come about? Honey didn't want Eliza to know her secret. Honey and Eliza always had lunch period together. Honey makes it her business not to eat lunch so as not to be seen by Eliza. Eliza notices that something wasn't right. Not a day would go by without Eliza seeing Honey at least once that day. But Eliza hasn't seen Honey at all the whole day. Honey went out of the school building to have lunch so as to avoid Eliza.

I feel bad about this, thought Honey. Why should I avoid Eliza? She's the only friend I've got. She would never tell anyone about my weirdness and the stupid freak that I am. I really don't want to tell her that I'm an insect. What would she think of me? How would she act toward me? Honey thought. "I don't think I could tell her about this. This is too deep. What about Jim? How much did he see? What if he tell what he had seen? I'm doomed," says Honey as she arrives at her front door.

Honey didn't see Jim or Eliza that day at school. When Honey steps inside the house, guess who was there to greet her at the door. Honey jaws literally hit the floor. She thought she had gone half of the day dodging Eliza. Honey forgets that Eliza knows where she lives and what time she arrives home from school.

"Hi!" says Eliza to Honey.

"Hi!" says Honey to Eliza.

"I miss you at school today; you hadn't come to lunch either," says Eliza.

"I went out to eat lunch," says Honey.

"You're not upset with me, are you? Asks Eliza.

"No, I'm not upset with you," says Honey.

"I could never be upset with you. You want to come inside of my room?" asks Honey. "I have something to tell you!"

The two go inside of Honey's room, and Eliza lets out a loud scream after being inside of Honey's room no more than three minutes. Honey feels a whole lot better knowing she couldn't dodge someone who knows her almost better than she knew herself. The two became even closer. Honey never had spoken to Eliza about the last time she went out with Jim or why they hadn't seen each other since.

Frank and Mary go away for their vacation the following weekend. Honey has a slumber party for her and Eliza at the house. At least eight people show up at the slumber party. Honey had even invited the two old ladies off the block who looked like they could enjoy some excitement in their life. Honey has plenty of games and food at the slumber party. While at the slumber party, Honey plays music, and everyone gets up to dance. At around twelve o'clock, the two elders decide to tell stories of their past.

Anthony arrives home from work.

"Oh! I had forgotten about your slumber party," says Anthony.

Eliza has a major crush on Anthony. Anthony doesn't pay Eliza any attention.

"Did you know that Jim was in the nuthouse?" says Anthony.

"No! I didn't have any idea," says Honey.

"He just got out," says Anthony.

"Someone came on the job telling that he was spooked. They say that he had run to a hospital one night saying some way-out crazy things just before he passed out. The funny thing is that he had some wet sticky stuff all over him. He had to be put inside of a straightjacket," says Anthony.

"Poor Jim!" says Eliza.

"I won't interrupt you all slumber party, I'm going to my room," says Anthony!

The next morning, everyone had awoken about ten that morning. Honey cooks breakfast for her guests. She had donuts and orange juice for everyone. Anthony got up to the smell of something cooking in the kitchen and he joins in.

Eliza likes every minute of Anthony's company. Everyone got prepared to leave and head toward home; Eliza was the last to leave the house, sitting there daydreaming at Anthony.

"Would you like to walk me home, Anthony?" asks Eliza.

"You're not that far away," says Anthony.

"Oh! Walk my friend home;" says Honey, "you see that she has a crush on you."

Eliza pushed Honey and tells her to be quiet.

"You think he does not know this?" says Honey. "All this time, you know, he knows that you are in love with him."

Anthony tells Eliza that he would walk her home as soon as he finishes eating. Eliza starts to blush as she waits patiently at the door for Anthony to walk her home.

Anthony is back soon to finish what little food he hadn't finish; he had taken the shortcut. This was one day Eliza tries to take the longest route home although Anthony was not trying to hear of it. While Anthony finishes the rest of his breakfast, Honey sat down at the table with him.

"Now as you were saying earlier about Jim's condition," asks Honey.

"Word is out that he is speechless, he hadn't spoken a word since that incident."

"I must say that was the night that I went out with him," says Honey. "That's the night that I had puked on him."

"Oh! So that explains everything," says Anthony! "You are the reason for this man's insanity."

"What are you trying to say," asks Honey, "that I drove the man crazy?"

"Well, no one but you could have done this to the poor guy," says Anthony. "You left the man speechless. You better hope that Jim stays speechless; if he ever talks, he has a lot to talk about."

The two sit looking into each other's eyes for a brief minute until Anthony says to Honey, "His mother tells the teacher that he would be returning to school real soon. He may never talk again, from what the doctors say. Sometimes they're not a hundred percent accurate," says Anthony.

"I shall hope not this time," mumbles Honey as she walks to her bedroom. The telephone rings, and it is Eliza.

"So what are you doing?" asks Eliza.

"Talking to you," says Honey.

"Oh! That's so right," says Eliza.

"Where is your brother?" asks Eliza.

"He's in the kitchen," says Honey. "I'm going to try and get some sleep, I'll call you tonight.

"Okay," says Eliza as she puts the receiver down slowly. Maybe I shouldn't call too much, Eliza thought to herself. "Am I bothering her too much? Should I limit my calling?

Eliza falls asleep wondering about this, so that night when Eliza awakes, she doesn't give Honey a call and the next morning as she usually does. Two nights have gone by without Eliza calling Honey. Honey calls Eliza to see if everything is okay with her. Eliza's mom picks up the telephone, and she tells Eliza to come get the telephone. Eliza is happy to know that it was Honey on the line; she could do nothing but smile.

"Are you okay?" asks Honey.

"I'm fine. I've been busy," says Eliza pretending.

"Oh! Are you busy now? I could call you back another time," says Honey.

"Oh No!" says Eliza as she almost drops the telephone hoping Honey doesn't hang up.

"What are you doing?" asks Honey.

"You want me to come over?" asks Eliza, "I'll be on my way if you want."

Eliza really missed Honey. It seems like the longest two days in her life without being around Honey. Honey felt somewhat bad to not be hearing from Eliza after that night.

"Yes, you could come over," says Honey. The two listen to the radio while playing a game until it was time for Eliza to leave. School was the next day. Honey walks Eliza to the door.

"I wish Anthony were here to walk me home again," says Eliza. "I think he is so awesome," she adds. "I'll call you as soon as I get inside of the door."

"I know you would," Honey says to Eliza.

Honey went to the washroom first, and then sat down to wait for Eliza's phone call. Eliza is just about to turn the corner from the shortcut to enter her house when she is grabbed from behind. Eliza has no idea what is happening to her at this moment. She starts to scream as she is grabbed by the mouth. Eliza is quickly pulled away into the woods far away from her house. The attacker held Eliza down on the ground as he starts to try to attack her. Eliza grabs at the man's face; she tries scratching his face. The attacker starts to hit Eliza in her face to protect him from being exposed. Eliza kicks the attacker with all of her might as she quickly tries to get away from the guy.

Eliza was too much for the guy; he decides to pull from his pocket a knife. The attacker puts his knife toward Eliza's throat and says to her, "If you don't calm down, I will kill you right here on the spot."

Eliza calms down for a minute. The guy rapes Eliza. When he is done, he reaches over with the knife to cut Eliza. Eliza manages to grab hold of a small brick hitting him in the face. Now this upsets the guy as he grabs his knife and begins stabbing Eliza in the face. The attacker is devastated as the blood runs down his face where Eliza had hit him to protect herself.

The attacker was very furious; he was in a rave. He picked up a bigger brick and begins to beat Eliza in her head with the brick. The attacker face was horrific after Eliza, dug her nails into the attacker face. This was what really upset the attacker. His face was scratched badly. Eliza made sure she left something to show where she had fought off her attacker. Eliza had once remembered a conversation that she and Honey had once had: Never let an attacker get away without leaving a mark somewhere. And the best place is his face where every time he looks in the mirror, he would think of you.

Eliza went out like a true fighter, she didn't give in. Eliza had actually broken a nail in the attacker's face to show that was how deep she was clawing at her attacker's face. Eliza grabbed Red's face as tightly as she could with her nails gripping his skin. The attacker felt like his flesh had just been ripped from his face. This angered him to the point that he took out his knife and cut off every one of Eliza's fingers. This didn't do. He decided to beat Eliza some more in the face with the brick as he smashed every bone in her face. Eliza went to her grave without giving up; she knew her attacker had no intention of letting her live, so she left evidence which Honey also had taught her.

The attacker's face starts to sting as he starts to sweat; before walking away from the crime scene, he kicks Eliza's dead body and runs through the woods. Eliza has gotten the attacker real good.

As the attacker leaves and turns the corner, Mary and Frank were arriving from late night grocery shopping. The guy tries to hide in the bushes as he pulls out an asthma pump. He has overexerted himself. But it's too late; Mary has taken a good glance at the attacker. He looks at her. The attacker tries to cover his face while hiding in the bushes. Mary quickly turns her head so that the attacker would not know she had seen him.

Mary tells Frank to "speed up, dear."

"What is the matter with you?" says Frank.

He had no idea why Mary tells him to speed up. Frank could not see the guy from his side of the car; he felt baffled. Mary jumps out of the car quickly and runs inside of the house hoping the guy doesn't realize that she had noticed him.

Frank comes inside of the house and asks Mary, "What's wrong, dear? You act as if you've seen a ghost."

"I've seen a man with blood on his face hiding in the bushes," Mary tells Frank.

Mary tells Frank that the guy had blood on his face with a white shirt on and how bloody the white shirt was. Honey still sits at the table waiting for Eliza to call her as Mary still goes on with her detail of what she has seen.

"What's wrong, Mom?" asks Honey.

"I've seen someone out back who looked like he's been cut up in the face," Mary explains.

Honey's eyes were big as she listens to her mother's story. Honey quickly grabs the telephone to call Eliza's house, and there was no answer.

"The guy ran away," says Mary, "you don't have to worry about him."

"I'm not worried about him, Mom, I worry about Eliza. She never called me when she got home." Honey decides to break for the door, and Frank grabs hold of her.

"Try calling Eliza once more; you're not going out there. That guy could be out there up to no good."

Honey calls Eliza's house once more, and Eliza's mom picks up the telephone.

"Hello, Mrs. Finch," says Honey.

"Has Eliza made it home yet?" asks Honey.

"No, dear, should she be heading toward this way?" asks Mrs. Finch.

"Yes, she had left long enough to have been there," says Honey.

"Oh my!" says Mrs. Finch, sounding devastated.

"I'll look around," says Honey to Mrs. Finch.

Honey sits for a brief minute as she wonders where Eliza could have gone! Honey feels that something was truly wrong and she was about to find out. Just as Honey goes toward the door, Anthony comes inside of the house.

"What's the rush?" asks Anthony. Eliza didn't make it home! "Do you want to go look for her respond Anthony?"

"Yes," responds Honey to her brother.

Mrs. Finch arrives at Mary's house, and she is very shaken up by Eliza being her only child and all. The police arrive at the house and begin to ask questions. The police decide to comb the area by starting through the woods. The neighborhood starts to get full of people coming from their houses to see about the commotion. Honey and Anthony walk the woods also to do their own investigating.

Mary had talked with two of the policemen to tell her version of what she had seen that evening. While in the woods, Honey hears noises. She begins to let her guard up until she realizes that it is one of the policemen cutting through the bushes. Honey goes toward another direction which leads toward Eliza's way although it is far back. Honey feels that she is being swayed to go in that direction. Honey leaves Anthony behind; she starts to run as fast as she could. Honey slows down as she looks over and sees her friend's nude body beaten real bad,

Honey walks toward her friend's body and drops down to her knees as she cries out. "Nooo, this is not so!" says Honey. Honey starts to go berserk as she looks at her friend Eliza lying there on the ground. Anthony catches up with Honey. He watches as Honey sits on the ground grieving her friend's death. Honey does not appear to be looking great at all to Anthony. Anthony doesn't dare go near his sister while she was in the state that she was in.

Honey sits on the ground as she watches her friend's body with dismay. She thought who would do something like this to my friend, my only friend. Anthony has seen his sister upset before, but not this upset. Honey body starts to stiffen up as she stood up to gain her composure; she couldn't do it. Something was holding her back, or was it her instinct of nature that reside in her holding her back? Anthony tells Honey not to do it; Anthony sees that Honey was about to come out of her shell.

"This is not the time," says Anthony to Honey,

"Don't do it please, Honey."

Honey's eyes start to change as she looks at her brother in a trance. Honey's eyes starts to twirl around in circles, and she starts seeing triple figures. Honey's eyes are not very focused at this moment. Honey stands over Eliza's body to protect her; she would not budge. Honey is about to experience a traumatic breakdown. Honey's eyes start to turn darker and much bigger as she begins to let out a light buzzing sound. Anthony stood way far from Honey, not knowing what is about to take place, although Anthony has no doubt that Honey would harm him.

Honey's body begins to tremble as she walks over closer to Eliza's body. Honey starts buzzing a little louder; Anthony looked around the woods to see if anyone is around. Anthony doesn't want anyone to see his sister the way she is; they might try to attack her out of fear thinking that Honey would harm one of them.

Anthony tries hard to calm Honey down although Anthony knows that he might just get the shock of his life. Anthony walks slowly to his sister; Anthony sees that his sister is in a deep trance. Honey has no recognition of what she's going through. The sound of bees gets louder as Honey gets madder. The policemen start to come out in the woods closer to where Eliza's body was at. There are at least twelve to fourteen police probing the woods. The policemen start to lie flat to the ground at the sound of bees. Honey has a small fragment of fur hair coming from her face.

Anthony couldn't believe his eyes; Anthony was more afraid for his sister than of his sister. Anthony realizes if the police see his sister this way, there was no telling what might take place. Anthony grabs Honey from behind and holds her as tightly as he could. Anthony wanted so much to bring his sister back; Honey had lost it for a brief minute just like she had done the night she was with Jim.

He whispers to Honey and says to her, "We will get through this; I promise you. We will get whoever did this to Eliza."

Anthony is still holding his sister as he feels a light stinging; it didn't matter to Anthony as long as he got the attention of his sister. Anthony didn't want the public to know about his sister's condition. So if taking a risk means getting stung, then he would take that risk. Anthony handles the situation just fine; Anthony is used to getting stung by his sister. I'm glad I didn't get the electric shock, he thought; I really had to calm Honey down. Anthony knows his sister well enough to know she would not hurt him, although Anthony stepped in right on time, before things had gotten worse. And believe that it does get worse. At that moment the police are not too many steps away from Anthony and Honey. Anthony is still holding on to his sister as the police come a little close.

The police say to Anthony, "We were afraid to step out from the woods; we thought that we had heard a swarm of bees out here, and they were pretty loud."

One of the policemen hits himself in the head thinking that bees are surrounding him, while two policemen are crawling on the ground trying to protect themselves from the bees that weren't in existence. Honey stands at the foot of Eliza's body; she doesn't want to leave Eliza's body. Honey feels like she would be abandoning Eliza. She says to herself, this is not over. I would not stop looking for who did this.

The coroner arrives at the scene. "Thank goodness you all came," says a policeman.

"If you had come a little sooner, I don't think you would have been able to take the body with you," says the policeman.

"Why is that?" asks one of the coroners.

"The young lady that was here was guarding the body and wouldn't bulge at all. It seems as though she was protecting the body of some sort," says the policemen.

"That's odd," says the coroner. "There is nothing left here at all but the shell when the soul leaves I wonder why would she want to stay with the body?"

"I have no idea," says the policeman.

The coroners quickly take Eliza's body away from the scene. Honey goes home, lies across her bed, and cries all night. That morning while in the shower, Honey thinks about Eliza. This feels so much like a dream.

"I wish someone would pinch me real hard so that I could wake up," says Honey, "from this crazy nightmare."

Honey step out from the shower as she stood in front of the mirror. Honey watches herself as she dries her body off. Honey notices some sticky substance coming from within her; she starts to wipe herself. Honey starts to get agitated with the remarkable stickiness as it slowly comes out of her body. Honey screams out so loud she wakes up her parents. Mary is at the door first. Mary knocks on the door to see what is wrong with Honey.

Mary opens the door and asks Honey, "Why were you screaming?"

Mary looks down on the floor, and there on the floor lies Honey in a fetal position.

"I have something sticky that's coming from out of me and I have no idea what this is," she says as she explains to her mother.

Mary explains the problem to Honey. "I really can't explain much. I truly believe that there is more to these episodes that you're going through. I just hope this doesn't affect your way of living your life," says Mary.

The neighbors were distraught over the incident involving Eliza's accident. The neighborhood was very tight for a couple of days; you couldn't tell if anyone resides in the neighborhood or not. Everyone kept their doors airtight and stayed inside. For the next couple of days, Honey is furious.

She says to her mom and dad, "I don't understand what's going on here."

"My friend who's also a person, who resides in the neighborhood, gets killed and we lock our doors as if we are scared. I mean it does give you something to think about. I've seen some people walk in groups just to go to the corner store," says Honey.

Frank tells Honey that the neighbor is in an uproar about this situation. Honey walks away from her parents to look out of the window. She has a lot on her mind.

Mary whispers to Frank and asks, "Did you know that Eliza's fingers were missing?"

"I had no idea!" says Frank to Mary.

"I really didn't want to say anything about this to Honey, dear."

"Do you think Honey knows about this?" says Frank.

"No," says Mary, "I found this out from Eliza's mother."

"Oh!" says Frank, "I don't think that you should say anything about this to Honey."

"Okay, dear, if you say so."

"You know this will bring something out of her. Honey hasn't been herself since Eliza's death," says Frank.

"I hate to see our child like this, Frank; she looks like she has bags underneath her eyes. Honey hasn't slept too well since Eliza's death," says Mary to Frank.

The night before the funeral, Mary has a rough time sleeping. Mary has a horrible nightmare that night; she has a dream of the guy who had killed Eliza. Mary tosses and turns all night. Honey is inside her room as she stares out of her window; she watches the stars. Honey does not sleep a wink at all that night; she just watches the stars until daybreak.

Meanwhile in the same city, not too far away, was Eliza's murderer. He is watching the news, doing the same normal thing just like a normal person would do. Criminals watch the news also. They too have to keep track of just how close the cops are on their tracks. Red has an idea that Mary had seen his face; he's not for sure although he's going to find out. Dirty Red has to find a way of knowing if he was seen by Mary or if his face or name is indicated in the murder, and he intends to find out.

Red turns on the television to watch. This was Dirty Red's informant to the murder as close as he could get. Dirty Red knows that he have to find out something; he's getting very afraid not knowing anything. Red has to find out just how much the media knows, as well as the public. Dirty Red lies across the bed as he watches the news. Before the news goes off, the media has a brief description of Dirty Red. No name although a brief description was all the information that the news media had to go on.

Mary has given the information to the police the day of the murder. Dirty Red also thinks that Mary has given information about him to the police. Dirty Red intends to shut Mary up permanently and anyone else who stands in the way. Dirty Red grabs some ice out of the refrigerator to fix himself a drink. He reaches into the freezer to pull out the ice tray, a plastic bag fell out of the freezer. Dirty Red picks up the plastic bag which contains Eliza's fingers and throws the bag back into the freezer as he makes a terrible noise.

Dirty Red has no regret for what he had done to Eliza; except for his badly scratched face. Eliza left her mark as deep as the words that would be placed on her headstone. When you look very close at Dirty Red's face, you would actually think that the letter E was on his forehead.

Dirty Red stood in the mirror as he had done earlier; he looks at his face. Dirty Red says to himself, I have to do something about these scars on my face. I will need some sort of makeup until I could get something done, seriously done.

Dirty Red calls his brother in New York to tell him about his problem and that he needs his help. The two talk on the telephone for five minutes when Greg asks Dirty Red what the big problem is.

"You have told me about the scratches that you have in your face; I assume you were in a major accident or you were in a cat's face, or could it just be you where in some bitch's face? Those are the three reasons so far that I could think of. And to top it off, you still have not told me the main problem why you're calling me. You call me saying that you had a problem! Now what's the real problem?" asks Greg.

"Well, I'm in deep over my head," says Dirty Red, "and I may need a place to hide out for a minute."

"Now we're getting somewhere," says Greg to his brother.

"I killed someone," says Dirty Red to his brother.

"You killed someone!" yells Greg.

"Yes, I've killed a girl," says Dirty Red.

"Have you smoked some crack, or are you just plain crazy in the damn head!" says Greg. "Red, what possess you to go out and do something like that?

"I don't know," answers Red.

"Well, you're better know if the police catch up to you," says Greg. "I'll come and get you tonight if I could. I've been watching the news, so you must be the person the police are looking for. You raped the girl, didn't you, man? You're out taking poo nanny again! What have I said to you about that dumb shit? I told you about taking something that's not yours! I have told you about that shit. Never take poo nanny from women! If she doesn't give it up, you go to another woman."

"Who would."

"There are plenty of women you could have, even if you have to pay for it," says Greg.

"Man, I'm never going to pay for no woman," says Red.

"Oh! You are willing to go to jail for a piece of poo nanny," says Greg, "either way your dumb ass would be locked the fuck up. So you're paying either way for some poo nanny. You are as dumb as your dumb-ass sound, dear dumb-ass brother of mines. Wake the hell up, I think I would come and get your dumb ass tonight before you do something else. In the meantime, you need to get up on what I'm doing; you need a few pointers."

Greg is one of the biggest pimps in New York.

"I'll let you use two of my whores," says Greg, "so maybe you wouldn't go around taking poo nanny anymore. Your ass was never locked up for that. I believe you've never learned only because you never was locked up for raping women. You know what; I'll come and get your dumb ass when I'm good and ready just for you being so damn dumb."

Greg clicks the phone down hard, hanging up on his brother. Red is very upset he starts to break up anything he could get his hand on. He stomps on the floor very hard that the neighbor who lives underneath him starts to hit the ceiling with her broom. Red stomps even harder when asked to stop the racket.

A lady yells up to Red and says to him to "Stop the racket before I come up there."

"You just bring your bad ass on up here and you'll be damn sorry!" says Red.

Red lies on the bed not knowing if and when Greg would come his way. Red starts to get nervous as he thought about every woman he'd ever raped and beaten. And never was he caught although each woman lived through his aggressive behavior. They were too afraid to turn Red in to the police. So he continues to abuse women this way. Red is afraid; he had never killed anyone before; it's just that Eliza was one of the rough ones. She had given him a run for his money, and she was not about to give up without a fight knowing that this would be her last night alive.

"I must think," says Red, "what am I going to do! I need to know more about what's going on."

Red turns on the television hoping that he would get more information than he had. While he was watching the news, the media reveal that the funeral arrangement is planned for tomorrow.

"Now, this is right up my alley. I need to get to the funeral. Now how would I do this? My face is truly fucked! I'll find a way," says Red.

Red walks toward the door of his apartment and peeks out the door. I need something to cover up my face so as to hide the scars in my face. Should I get makeup to cover up my face like my mom used to do when my dad blacked her eyes a couple of times?

Maybe seeing what his dad done to his mother explains the aggressive behavior Red has with women. Red starts to close his door when he heard the woman under him whispering to another woman. He wants so bad to ask for makeup. He knows that most women carry a little makeup. Red steps out of the apartment to eavesdrop a little closer. He could see the two women now that he's closer. One woman walks away to go to her apartment, leaving the other woman alone.

What should I do? Does she live alone? How I would get her to open the door? I'll hide on the side then I'll jump on her as soon as she opens the door. Red finally finds a solution. Red goes toward the woman's apartment and knocks on the door. Without answering the door, she opens the door thinking that her neighbor had come again. Red quickly pushes the woman into her apartment and throws her to the floor and begins punching the woman in the face until she's unconscious.

Red runs to the bedroom, knocking things off of her dresser, and then he goes toward the bathroom, looks into the medicine cabinet to see if he could find any kind of woman's makeup to cover up his face. Red was very desperate. He has to cover up his scars so he could hide out at the funeral. Red finds a makeup bottle which looks to be very old and dried up. Red returns to his apartment to put the makeup on his face. He has added water into the bottle, and that helps a little. Red has put makeup on his face to see actually how he would look, and it was perfect as long as he didn't sweat.

The next day, Red arrives at the funeral two hours before service has begun. Red walks inside of the funeral to see if anyone was inside. The site was clear; he doesn't see anyone inside of the funeral, not even the coordinator.

"I've guess they're in this big place somewhere," says Red. He walks over to Eliza's body and he says to her, "It's all because of you that my face is the way it is." He took out the knife he had once use on Eliza. "I guess I'm here to return the favor," says Red, and he walks out of the funeral's home to wait for the other arrivals.

Red hides in the bushes waiting for others to arrive. The first to arrive was Eliza's mother. Then others pull up in their cars soon after. Just then Mary and Frank pull up in the car with Anthony and Honey right behind them in a brand-new car that Anthony had just purchased yesterday. The family walks inside of the church to pay their respect.

Red walks over to Frank's car; he says to himself, "Yes! This is the same car the two of them was driving that night." Red starts to write down the license plate number. Red leaves Frank a note left it on the windshield of the car as he walks away from the car without being seen by anyone.

Red makes it home without being seen hoping that maybe Greg would have some good news since he hasn't arrived last night to pick him up for New York. As soon as Red returns to the house, the telephone rings, and it's Greg.

"I'll be there in ten minutes. I'm not too far away from you. "You haven't gotten yourself in any more trouble, have you, dumb ass?" says Greg to his brother. "Make sure you bring everything that is needed with you, I'm not returning back unless it's very important; concerning our mother, that would be the only reason for me to come back here."

Red loads up his belongings, which weren't much. He is ready when Greg arrived. The two quickly left for New York.

As everyone goes to be seated at the funeral, Mrs. Finch walks up toward the casket to take a look at her daughter, and she screams out loud as she fell to the floor and fainted. Mrs. Finch shakes up the entire funeral. The funeral director is just as devastated to see what he'd seen. The rest of the guests are too upset at seeing Mrs. Finch's reaction to go up toward the casket to see just what had Mrs. Finch out like a light.

The coordinator helps Mrs. Finch from the floor and looks over in the casket and quickly closes the casket. Mrs. Finch is coming to as she starts to scream out again.

"We are going to postpone the funeral for an hour until we could do some new arrangement, "says the coordinator as they took the body out from the room.

"What's going on here?" Mary asks.

"I have no idea," the lady next to Mary answers.

Honey and Anthony decide to go outside to get some air and to get away from the grief-stricken guests. Honey walks over toward the car to sit on the hood and gather her thoughts as she was truly hurting inside.

"Don't go through one of your spells," says Anthony.

"I don't think I've have the hang of my situation," says Honey.

Anthony notices the note on the hood of the car; he reaches to lift the note from the car and begins to read the note.

Honey asks Anthony, "What is the note about?"

Anthony hands the note to Honey. She reads the note and gets pretty upset behind this. She tears the note to many pieces before thinking.

"Why did you do that?" asks Anthony.

"What are you talking about?" Honey says to Anthony.

"There could have been some fingerprints on the note."

"Oh! I was not thinking, Anthony. I'm so sorry, I really weren't thinking. I'm just so mad right now."

"Don't worry about it, the jerk would slip sooner or later," says Anthony.

Mary and Frank come from out the church as the two walk over toward the car. Frank notices the expression on Honey's face. He walks over and says to her, "Everything would be all right as soon as this nightmare is over."

"You know what someone has done," says Frank, "they had the audacity to carve letters across Eliza's forehead."

"That's what the commotion was about. Now what crazy-ass person would tamper with the deceased body like that?" says Anthony. He storm away.

"Did that boy just cuss?" says Frank.

"I don't think he realizes that he had cussed," says Honey to her parents.

Honey and Anthony have the utmost respect for their parents. Never throughout their life, had Mary and Frank had a problem out of those two.

Honey walks over to her brother and says to him, "Did you know what you had said back there?" asks Honey.

"What did I say back there? I don't remember; I'm very confused and upset about this whole damn situation," says Anthony.

"That's what you did back there around our parents, you cussed again," Honey says to her brother as she giggles trying to control her laugh. "I know you're upset."

"You mean to say I slip up!"

"Oh yes, you slip up all right and you just did it again; don't get too carried away, they're going to let you slide with this one," says Honey.

"What are we going to do? Asks Anthony.

"Well, I really don't know," says Honey, "since I screw up every proof that we ever had in our possession. Should we tell our parents?" asks Honey.

"I don't think that we should say anything to the both of them just yet," says Anthony.

"Let's just keep this a secret just for a minute until we could find the ass wipe. Now I earn that I needed to get that out of me," says Honey, referring to the cussword she had said.

The two walk over toward their parents and ask if the four should be going inside to see if the service has begun.

While walking inside, Mary hits Anthony upside the head saying to him, "I owe you one. You are pretty upset to cuss like that." She smiles at her son and gives him a hug.

After the funeral and burial, the family goes home. Later that evening, Mary and Honey go to Mrs. Finch's house to sit with her. From time to time, the family would go over to visit Mrs. Finch to keep her company. Some nights, Honey would stay nights over.

Three years have gone by and the police had not come any closer to finding Eliza's attacker. Eliza's case went to the cold-case file; the detectives never like it when this happens. Anthony and Honey have moved out from their parents' home and are on their own. Anthony is married with one child and one on the way while Honey is still single. Now Honey doesn't know if it's by force or by choice that she's alone.

"I'm damned if I do and I'm damned if I don't," says Honey as she looks out of her window.

The family doesn't stay too far away from one another; they visit at least twice a week. Honey goes to the cemetery where Eliza was buried and visits often. She has run into Mrs. Finch quite a few times, and Mrs. Finch was happy to see her every time. This helps Mrs. Finch a lot, knowing that not only she cared and loved her daughter. And that she was not forgotten about after being laid to rest. Until later, Mrs. Finch was laid to rest soon after.

Honey watches the bees as they make a home for themselves. She sees that the children are playing close by as long as the children play away from the tree. Honey walks toward the kitchen and picks up her pooch whom she named Booby and whom she loves very much. Honey grabs a nectarine from the refrigerator and starts to eat it. Honey hears the children who were out playing scream. She quickly jumps from her chair and runs out to see what was going on with the children.

Bees were flying and surrounding the children; Honey quickly stands out and manifests her body to signal to the bees. The bees stop attacking the children and went toward Honey as she stuck her hands out toward the bees and signals them toward her. The bees surround Honey as if they were communicating with her. The bees were in the air surrounding Honey without touching her body. The bees were in a trance at Honey's command. Honey was part of a colony which the bees derive on Honey, and she has the power to communicate with any bee that's out.

The children were protected. As the four children run away to tell their parent about what had happened to them, Honey decides to leave the house to go to her gym which she had owns for a year now. Honey loves to work out; the guys loved to see when Honey work out. Honey has a big gym, full of equipment that the guests love using when they arrive at the club. Honey is also the instructor of her club; and the guys love for her to instruct them.

Honey hasn't been out on a date since Jim. Honey had seen Jim about a month ago; he's back speaking although he had nothing to say to Honey. It was like he was still speechless. There is this one guy who follows Honey around like the puppy she has at home. He wants pretty much to be with Honey. Honey done told the guy over again that she's not interested in a date or anything of that sort.

Honey is still a virgin, and she would remain a virgin, which she has no idea of this although she would soon find out. After the incident with Jim some years ago, she says to herself that she would never go out with a man again. So she thought. Honey has seen quite a few guys that had turned her head when she was at the age of puberty. It's just that she wants to stay pure and fresh as a virgin although she feels her body is yearning for some attention.

Honey doesn't know how to handle her body whenever nature starts to come, meaning when she's excited without a man, Honey starts to become overheated. She removes her clothes and jumps quickly in the shower. This is how she controls her sexual pleasure, by cooling herself off.

Honey could not ever show affection for a man sexually. The man would be in grave danger if and when they become physically, sexually connected with Honey. Honey would never forget the episode she had experience.

After closing the club, Honey stops at her parents' house to check up on her mother. Mary had been sick recently, so the family had been visiting her every so often. When Honey arrives at her parents' home, Frank and Mary were sitting on the couch. Looking through some of their photo albums, Honey walks inside of the house and sits right next to her mother. The three sit looking at the photo album when Anthony walks inside of the house.

Anthony has a little girl aged two; his wife is four months pregnant. The two are hoping for a boy this second time around. The family all begin to look at the photo album and enjoy the evening until Honey runs across a picture of her and Eliza together standing against a tree. Honey begins to cry, and Mary holds her daughter.

"I think it's time to put the photo album up," says Frank as he reaches for all four of the photo albums.

That evening while they are watching the news, there is another murder, and the police aren't sure if the murders were connected. Honey and Anthony start to look at one another as if the two were thinking the same thing at that moment. Honey is the first to say what is on her mind.

"You all remember while attending Eliza's funeral, while you two were inside, there was a note on the windshield of your car threatening that if you say anything to the police about anything, the person would come back and kill you too."

"I did say something to the police," says Mary.

"Well, obviously the attacker didn't think much of it, he knows that you may have seen him but didn't see him that good," says Honey.

"What about the woman he had beaten up pretty bad that was in a coma for three days? Yes, they did say that she had come out of the coma. She didn't tell them much to go on. When the police came back to the hospital to ask about him, she had nothing to say. The woman was too out of it, she had blunt trauma to the head pretty bad," says Anthony.

"So the police had nothing to go on," says Frank, "the woman died right after."

"Did the police think that it was the same person," asks Anna, Anthony's wife.

"We never found out," Frank responds.

"You mean to tell me. All this time the two of you never told me about a note on our car from the killer himself," says Mary to Honey and Anthony getting back to her children.

"We didn't want you to have anymore nightmares," says Anthony.

"Well, this means that the guy is still out there, somewhere," asks Anna. "I bet any kind of money that this guy has to be the one," says Anna.

"Dad, do you think that you could go to the authorities and find out more," asks Anthony.

"You should be able to do better than that!" says Anna.

"What do you mean?" asks Anthony.

"Ask her parents," says Anna, "maybe the police gave the family more additional information."

"I doubt that, and if the police did, Mrs. Finch went to her grave with the information," says Frank to Anna.

"Oh! That is so terrible to hear!" says Anna. "This woman had to endure such pain. Does a person who kills know what kind of damage that it have on a person, loved one who's left behind to endure the pain? You not only hurt the one that is dead. It's like you have also killed the person who has to live through the ordeal, the pain, the heartache. It's like a part of you done actually died with that person. And you are never the same anymore. I know, my brother was killed in a robbery. They not only robbed him, they turned around and killed him for three dollars. A lot of petty thieves out there. If you're going to rob someone, at least let the person live, he's been insulted enough by the robbery alone."

"I'm sorry," says Anna, "if I'm coming off this way but I don't care for those kinds of people in my life. My mother still grieves my brother right to this day. I'm grieving also, but my mother's hurt is much deeper than my hurt. I sat with my mother one day and she says to me, 'You never want to loose a child.' She tells me 'It feels just like someone has stabbed her in the heart.' The only way to get rid of the pain is the day that she parted. A lost is a tremendous hurt and no one should have to go through this. But we all would have to take a trip on that journey someday."

Everyone is silent at that moment until the telephone rings, and Mary was first to jump up to get the telephone, which amazed everyone in the house.

"What a full recovery," says Frank to Mary as they all laugh at Frank's remark.

While living it up in New York, Red and Greg were having a nice time. Red has no remorse whatsoever about what he'd done in the past, nor has he thought about it. Once Red made it to New York, Greg had two of his whores waiting for him. Greg has so many whores; they respect him, never giving him any problems.

Red holds Eliza's fingers in a silver steel container every now and then. He would think about disposing Eliza's fingers but was afraid of someone finding them. So he holds on to them not just for that purpose. Red thinks that holding on to Eliza's fingers was his way of punishing her for the marks on his face. Red is very aggressive when it comes down to how to treat a woman.

Red hadn't changed a bit, not with the line of work he's doing. Two of Red's whores were in a heated fight while he was in the shower, and Red comes out from the shower stark naked.

Red charges at the two women and says to them both, "I'm the only one who fights around here. If I catch you two lolly gagging again, I swear I'll have to cut your booty holes out. One more time, you two have one more time!"

Red was not playing with the women; Red is serious when it comes to his money. The two women go out of the house to go to work for Red seeing the expression on his face. They knew that Red meant business at that moment.

Greg on the other hand has his women on their toes like clockwork. Greg has eleven whores whom he has on the street every day of the week except Sunday. This happens to be one of Greg's days, when he would have quality time with his women. This is the day that he would be catered to all day. Red tries so hard to be like his brother, Greg, although the two are somewhat alike. The two have no respect for women; this is how the two were so much alike.

Honey sits in her bedroom while glancing out the window. Booby jumps into Honey's lap wanting Honey's attention while Honey daydreams. Honey decides to take Booby out for a walk. While walking, Honey runs into an attractive young guy around her age. The two appear to be interested in one another as the two exchange telephone number. Honey arrives home, feeds Booby and herself and takes a shower, and fell fast asleep. The next morning, the telephone rings, and it was Frank calling.

"I'm sorry, dear, for waking you up this early. It's your mother, she's gotten worst. I need you and Anthony to meet me at the hospital."

"Okay, I'll see you there," says Honey. Honey calls Anthony and tells him about their mother.

Frank had arrived at the hospital with Mary. As soon as she was being admitted, Honey arrives.

Later that evening, the doctor had determined what was wrong with Mary after examining her and doing lab work. Nearby and not too far away was Mrs. Rogers. She was hit by a car while standing on a bus stop waiting on a bus by a drunk driver who was later captured five minutes after. Mrs. Rogers happens to be Greg and Red's mother. Greg and Red have gotten word about their mother, and the two had to leave from New York to see about their mother at the hospital.

Red had surgery done to his face three years ago so as not to be noticed by anyone. Red and Greg arrive at the hospital.

Frank and the kids have been at the hospital for at least four hours visiting Mary when Frank says to Mary, "I have to be leaving, but I'll definitely be back tomorrow. I have to get to work, dear!" Frank reached over to kiss his wife on the lips. Honey and Anthony do the same, and the three leave to head toward the parking lot of the hospital.

Around the corner and two doors down are Red and Greg in a room visiting their mother?

"Hello, Mom," says Greg as he tried to get his mother's attention. Mrs. Rogers holds on to Greg's hand very tightly. She had not seen Greg in about five years. Greg tells his mother that Red was with him. Mrs. Rogers squeezes Greg's hand again. Mrs. Rogers had gained some consciousness since that morning of the accident. The doctor walks into the room and asks about the identity of the two young men.

"We are the sons of Mrs. Rogers," says Greg to the doctor.

"Okay! Were getting somewhere. I need for one of you to sign some papers if it's okay," says the doctor.

Red is the first to jump up and grab the paper to sign.

"Okay! It's not that serious for you to be acting the way you are. We are both her sons," says Greg.

Although Greg was Mrs. Roger's favorite, Red has known this all his life. Right now, Red feels that he had to show Greg he's capable of showing him off some kind of way. While in New York, Greg is the top guy. Red didn't care for that much.

Greg says to Red, "Why are you so quick to jump! You might have signed your death warrant, fool." Red tries to take the paper which he had sign from the doctor although the doctor has no idea of what's going on.

The doctor leaves the room, leaving Greg and Red to carry on where he left out on.

Red storms out of the room and walks outside to head for the parking lot, where the car is parked. Greg catches up to Red telling him to slow down so he could talk with him.

"The only thing I want you to do is play it safe, dude, we're back here in the town where a murder took place, which I had no parts of, remember. So don't be quick to jump at nothing, dear brother of mines!"

"Whatever," says Red.? Now this angers him also that Greg has to be in charge.

Honey walks passed the two while Red flicks a cigarette to the ground, almost hitting Honey on the stilettos she was wearing. Honey looks in the direction from which the cigarette had come. There was Greg and Red standing with a smile ten inches wide. Greg elbows Red in the side telling him "to watch yourself before you burn the fine lady," trying to get Honey's attention. Honey walks on by as she comes closer to her car. Greg stays closer to her.

"Damn, man! I know you're not that desperate for some ass!" yells Red to Greg.

"No! I see what I like. I would most definitely leave my whores for this one, says Greg.

"Now! I know damn well you done lost your freaking mind," says Red.

"She looks fine as hell," says Greg as he walks over to Honey's car trying to hold a conversation.

"I know damn well Greg is not losing his touch," says Red to himself as he sat down inside of their car to use his asthma pump. When Red is finished, he throws the pump out the window of the car.

Honey notices Red's action and says to him, "You are trashy," as she picks the pump from the ground and disposes of it in its proper place.

"May I ask your name if you don't mind?" asks Greg.

"Honey is my name!"

"Honey! It fits you to a T," says Greg, trying not to sound too eager.

"I must be leaving," says Honey.

"Could I leave you with my number?" says Greg.

"I don't think so," says Honey.

"Don't be that way," says Greg.

"I'm not interested," says Honey. Honey starts her car to let Greg know that she's ready to take off with him while his body is practically halfway inside of her car. "Excuse me," says Honey as she drives slowly away.

Greg starts to run with the car as Honey drives off. Greg writes his telephone number down and tries throwing the number inside of Honey's car. Honey shook her head as she drives away, leaving Greg standing looking very stupid. Red is loving every minute of Greg's stupidity.

"Did you get the name of that donkey who just kicked you all up in your ass?" says Red as he laughs at his brother. "You've never been turned down before but today is your lucky day." Red picks up the piece of paper Greg had written his number on.

"Man! She was a fine-ass bitch! Excuse my language," says Greg.

"What!" says Red.? "I know you're not saying excuse you for what you just said about a woman you just met," says Red.

Greg is about five feet seven inches tall and is a very attractive man, and he knows this. Greg is very sure of himself never having a problem with any woman on this planet.

"I guess you are not the shit anymore," says Red to Greg.

"I'm still the shit and always would be," says Greg as the two walk toward Greg's car.

"You feel real shitty right now, don't you? Asks Red. "Let me do the honor of wiping the shit off of your shoe."

"Leave me the fuck alone before I turn your ass in to the police myself," says Greg.

"Your ass better be glad that they didn't have a reward out for your ass. I would have been turned your sorry ass into the police." Now. Red is silent at that moment, not saying a word. Greg arrives at his mother's house still not saying a word to his brother Red for cracking the donkey joke on him, although it was the truth. Greg just cannot believe that he was turned down; now this puzzled him plus angers him!

Honey listens to her CD as she drives to the cemetery to visit the grave site of Eliza. While driving, she hears Eliza's favorite song on the radio of someone's car who drove past her.

"This is very odd," says Honey as she pulls over into the cemetery.

Honey stops at the flower shop to purchase a bouquet of flowers for Eliza's grave site. Honey sits at the grave site for nearly two hours before her departure. Honey's thoughts of anger have come over her again as she thinks of Eliza. Honey had to pull herself together as she leaves the grave site of Eliza. While driving, Honey had to pull over toward the side of the road to restrain herself. She cries profusely as she relives that night of Eliza's death. Honey drives home to her house as she opens the door, Booby greets her at the door.

"How's my big boy doing?" says Honey to her dog. Honey fed her dog and went upstairs to take a shower. The next morning, Honey decides to go to the hospital again to visit her mother. Anthony had made it to the hospital that morning. While going into the hospital, Honey meets her dad at the elevator and the two rides the elevator together. While turning the corner to Mary's room, Honey and Frank have missed Greg and Red as the two of them turn into their mom's room which is a couple doors down.

Frank tells Mary that she is feeling much better.

"I wonder would the doctors release you today," says Honey to Mary.

"I shall hope so," says Mary, "I'm tired of being coop up in this hospital."

The doctor walks inside of the room and says to Mary, "Today is your unlucky day."

"Why is that?" says Mary.

"We would be sending you home today; you won't have the pleasure of staying with us another day," says the doctor jokingly. Everyone starts to laugh at the doctor as he asks Mary to sign some papers.

Nearby in the room where Greg and Red visit their mom, the doctors give the two some disturbing news, that their mom would not be coming home at all.

"Mrs. Rogers does not have too long to live," says the doctor.

"I'm very sorry to inform you two of this. I wish I had better news for you," the doctor says to Red and Greg.

Greg walks out of the room to have a moment to himself, not wanting to accept what he had just heard from the doctor. Red stayed and held on to his mother's hand. Honey decides to go out to get a drink from the water fountain. While drinking at the water fountain, Honey sees Greg sitting down in the waiting area. Greg doesn't see Honey. Honey notices that Greg is crying. Honey is a very sensitive person; although Greg came on to Honey forcefully, she feels some sadness and wants to know why he sits crying.

Honey sits next to Greg. Greg has no idea who is sitting next to him until she hands Greg a napkin. Greg says thank-you and looks up and was very startled to see who it was.

"What's the matter?" says Honey.

"My mother has not too long to live," says Greg to Honey.

"That's terrible," says Honey. Honey had felt so bad for Greg. Honey tells Greg that she's about to go to her mother's room. "I hope you get better," says Honey to Greg.

Greg sits in the chair and puts on a more serious cry since he has gotten Honey's attention. He might as well take it far, just maybe she would accept his telephone number this time if he is so lucky. Honey feels bad for the guy; she walks back toward Greg as she writes down her telephone number. Red walks out from the room to tell Greg that their mother had just taken her last breath. Honey's heart had just melted.

The doctor walks out of the room and says to Greg, "Your mother had just expired," not knowing that Red had informed him already of his mother's passing. Greg bursts out into tears at that moment, and Honey tries to console him as the two sit down together.

"There is a chapel on the first floor of the building if the two of you would like to have some privacy," Honey says to Greg. She tells them that she was about to part from them both so she could be with her family. Honey gives Greg the piece of paper with her telephone number on it. Red's eyes went buck wide as he actually sees what had just taken place. Honey walks away to be with her family.

Greg says to Red, "All you have to do is put on the sad face, and it works every time."

"What! Use our mother's death to get what you want?" says Red.

"No! I just played along with the tune by rubbing it in deeper. I had no idea that she was around me," says Greg. I was hurt at that moment and I'm still hurt about our mother's passing. Honey just happens to be standing nearby."

"I just put the pressure on then you come out and that was all she wrote," says Greg as he looked at the piece of paper he gotten from Honey.

Honey returns to the room where her family was. At this time, the family is ready to leave the hospital. Upon leaving the hospital, Honey runs into one of her longtime schoolmates whom we will call Tim. He was really called Chewy because of his sharp double teeth. Honey gives Tim a hug as the two talks for a brief moment. Anthony drives up on the way out of the parking lot as he's about to leave he had noticed Honey talking to someone. Anthony drives up to Honey to get a closer look at the guy who she was talking to. Anthony gives a big smile as he got closer to them both.

"What's happening?" Anthony says as he steps out from the car to shake Tim's hand. Honey smiles at Anthony; she could see the look on Anthony's face, he really wants to laugh out loud every time Tim opens up his mouth. Honey gives Tim another hug and proceeds toward her car.

"I'll see you later, Chewy, I mean, Tim! Sorry about that." Honey starts to snicker at her brother's remark.

While at their parents' house, Honey says to Anthony, "Why did you have to embarrass Tim the way you did? You know he hates when he's called that name." The two start to laugh again at the mention of Tim's name.

"No, that's not nice," says Mary to Honey and Anthony. Anthony gets a telephone call on his cell phone, and it was his wife calling, telling him to get home before his dinner gets cold.

"I'm about to head on home," says Anthony.

"Yeah! The boss has spoken," says Honey to Anthony.

"We know what that telephone call was about." Anthony smiles at Honey as he gives his mother a kiss on the cheek and tells her he'll call her later.

"Mind your business," says Anthony to Honey as he left the house.

"I guess I'll be on my way," says Honey to her parents.

As soon as Honey arrives home, her main man Booby greets her at the door. Honey checks her caller ID and her voice massages as she takes off her clothing. She has at least thirty-seven messages and eighty-two calls. As Honey checks her messages, at least fifteen were from Greg.

"Damn! I'm wondering now, did I make the wrong mistake at feeling sorry for this guy?" she mumbles to herself as she goes up to take a quick shower stark naked dropping pieces of her clothing on the stairs. The telephone rings once more while Honey was in the shower. It was Greg on the line calling Honey again.

Red sits as he watches Greg call Honey on the telephone. "Have you realized just how many times you have called this one lady," says Red to Greg. "And you have not called, not one time to check up on your whores back at New York. They might be fucking up on you, man! That's your money, and you worry about a woman you hardly know for a minute," says Red.

"Stay out of my business," says Greg to his brother as he persists in using his cell phone once again.

"Okay!" says Red, "I'll do just that! I'm so glad you have unlimited minutes," says Red as he mumbles to himself.

Just as Honey lies down to rest, the telephone rings once more.

"Hello!" says Honey.

"What's up?" says Greg.

"Nothing much," says Honey.

"I've been trying to reach you," says Greg.

"You don't say," said Honey to Greg.

"I'm not trying to stalk you or nothing, would it be possible if I could take you out to dinner tomorrow?" asks Greg.

"I think I could find time," says Honey.

Red leans against the wall repeating every word which comes from Greg's mouth. Greg turns away trying to ignore his brother's sarcasms.

"I'm pretty tired right now to talk, but we could finish this conversation tomorrow," says Honey as she says good-by to Greg.

"Okay, I'll talk with you tomorrow," says Greg.

Honey lies on the couch and turns on the television for a quick second as she nods off to sleep. Honey had a terrible dream, surrounded by dark eerie shadows which she just cannot make out. She falls to the ground helpless trying very hard to get up. As she tries, a force is holding her down. Honey tosses and turns in her sleep. She manages to get up from the ground and run as fast as her legs could carry her. Honey is pretty much afraid; what is this thing that's tormenting her while she sleeps? Honey continues to run a little faster, and she appears to be moving very slowly no matter how fast she was running. Honey falls to the ground once more. This has got to be a dream, Honey tells herself as she tries to get up from the ground.

Quickly the figure comes at Honey; she starts to crawl realizing that she can't walk for some reason. Honey can't seem to get up from the ground. Just as Honey gets halfway up from the ground, she is knocked back down to the ground with such force. It's very dark and she cannot see a thing only the dark shadow that dances in the darkness while laughing. Honey gets very excited, and she begins to change only to still be frightened by the figure that she cannot make out in the dark. Honey grabs hold of the tree to pull herself up, but she's knocked down again. Honey tried hard to use her strength to get up, but the figure is much too strong for her, so Honey gives in to resisting. As the figure surrounds her, Honey balls up into a fetal position, scared as she has ever been. The figure comes closer to Honey and leans over her body. Honey is very afraid. Honey opens her eyes to see that the figure she sees is Red all covered with bees.

The bees come off of him on to Honey. The bees appear to be tamed to attack Honey. Honey covers her face as she tries so hard to protect herself from the bees. Honey decides to open her eyes, and she realizes that she cannot, it's because her eyes are not there at all. The bees have eaten them, and she has nothing but the socket of her eyes.

No! Red has her eyes in his hand and runs away with them. Honey lifts herself up from the ground with the help from a headstone. Honey backs away as she stands up on her two feet for as long as she could until she realizes whose headstone it was. The headstone reads Eliza Ann Finch. Honey starts to scream. The more she screams, the louder Red laughs at Honey as he disappears into the wood. Honey was so afraid as she awoke kicking and screaming. As she screams, the dog barks louder. After Honey had realized that she was dreaming, Booby jumps on Honey's lap and starts to howl.

Honey knows now that her dream was trying to tell her something. "What it is she doesn't know but she's aiming to find out?" Honey says to herself as she walks to her kitchen. She goes into the refrigerator to eat her nectarine early in the morning; she wants a nectarine. She says to herself, "I really need to do a little grocery shopping."

The telephone rings, Honey took her time as she walks over toward the phone to look down at the caller ID hoping that it was not Greg on the phone.

"Good," says Honey as she picks up the receiver. It was her brother, Anthony.

"What's up with you this bright early morning?" Anthony says to her, sounding very cheerful.

"Well, somebody is feeling real good." says Honey.

"What's the matter with you," asks Anthony.

"I had a terrible nightmare," says Honey.

"What was it about?" says Anthony.

"I was covered up with bees over my body," says Honey, "and I was very helpless and couldn't defend myself; that was the worst part of the dream."

"Ooh! Now we know that you were truly dreaming," says Anthony as he jokes with her.

"I'm about to hang up on you," says Honey.

"I'm just kidding with you," says Anthony.

"Guess who was in my dream?" asks Honey to Anthony.

"I don't have time for guessing," says Anthony.

"The brother of the guy that I have a date with tonight," says Honey.

"He was very eerie," says Honey, "and he was covered with bees, and he kept on knocking me to the ground. "And after this, I realized that I'm at the grave site of Eliza," says Honey.

"What! Now that is very weird. So what do you think this means?" asks Anthony.

"What I think is I'm never going to trust Greg's brother, although he gave me the creeps when I first seen him. I have a date with his brother tonight," says Honey.

"Don't go," says Anthony. "You sure you are not going to slob all down this one throat."

"You see, I really don't find that to be funny," says Honey, "and besides, I promised him that I would go out with him. "His mother passed away and I felt so bad for him," says Honey.

"What a way to go," says Anthony.

"Okay," says Honey, "I'll talk to you later," she says as she hangs up the telephone. Later that even while grocery shopping, Honey runs into another one of her schoolmates.

"Hello, Honey," says Maria as she puts her grocery on the line.

Hello! Maria said Honey, standing at the check out counter.

"Are you going my way?" asks Maria. My brother just called; he can't make it, could you give me a lift?" says Maria.

"No problem," says Honey. The two walk toward the parking lot together, and Maria asks Honey about her friend Eliza.

"Did they ever find Eliza's murderer?" asks Maria.

"No! Not at all," says Honey.

"I heard that on the night of Eliza's murder, there was this woman who had seen this man with scratches all over his face and he was bleeding very badly. She had asked the guy if he needed help, but he refused and pushed her down as he ran down the street into the bushes."

"When did you hear that?" asks Honey.

"At the time of the murder," says Maria.

"Why didn't anyone bring up that information at the time of Eliza's murder," says Honey.

"I have no idea," says Maria.

"That year everyone were very frightened and that leaked out when it didn't suppose to. I heard my mother talking on the telephone and you know I couldn't repeat what I've heard inside of my own house," says Maria.

"I guess you are right," says Honey as she put the groceries inside of the trunk.

Honey has driven Maria home, and the two exchange telephone numbers. Later that evening, Honey went on her date with Greg; and he was ever so grateful. The two were at a Mexican restaurant which Honey loves. She loves the spices of Mexican flavor. The two talk about their line of work while Greg claims to be a consultant for a law firm. The two have finished dining out, and Greg wants to continue the date, so he asks Honey if he could take her to the movie since the night was still young. Red sits at his mother's house bored without anything to do, so he decides to call to New York to harass the whores.

"Are you out making my money?" Red asks.

"Who is this?" says Myra.

"This is your pimp," says Red.

"I don't think so," says Myra.

"Who is this?" says Red.

"I'm Myra," she says to Red.

"Oh! My beg! You're one of my brother's whores. Put my whore on the telephone," says Red.

"Hello," says Alicia.

"What's up?" says Red. "Are you making my money?"

"Yes, I am, Daddy, when are you coming home?" she asks Red.

"Real soon, baby, real soon. "I'm bored as hell and I need some like right now," Red says to her.

"I'll give it to you, Daddy," says his whore. "I'll never deprive you of sex."

"I know damn well you won't, I'll take it If I have to," says Red.

Red want to get his point across to his whores, letting the girls know who was in charge.

After the movie, Honey tells Greg that she's very tired and she needs to go home and get her some rest. Greg is not ready for Honey to leave not knowing if he would ever see her again.

"Could I see you again?" he asks Honey as she proceeds to walk away toward her car.

Honey starts to stretch her body as she felt a little stiffness from sitting. Greg watches her body as she stretched, loving every minute. As Honey walks away, Greg follows right behind her just like her own dog would. Honey realizes that she has Greg in the palm of her hand so she wants to test him by asking him a question.

"I want to know where your girlfriend is," asks Honey.

"I don't have one," says Greg.

"Are you sure?" asks Honey.

"No! I do not. Do you want to be my woman?" asks Greg.

"You do not have to lie to me," says Honey.

"I'm not, why would I lie to you?" says Greg.

For many of reasons," says Honey. "Why should I believe you?" says Honey.

"Because I really care about you," says Greg.

"Just be yourself," says Honey, "Just be who you really are."

"You know what; I really am being myself," says Greg, "which amazes me. Despite the bumps I had to come across, I'm really being myself with you."

Strange as it seems, Greg was being himself. It's just that he had to cover up his line of work to make himself more prevailing to Honey. Greg really does like Honey; she is the kind of woman he would love to spend his life with, so to speak. Greg really didn't want Honey to know that he has at least eleven whores who work for him night and day.

"What about you?" asks Greg?

"I'm pretty much single, and I intend to keep it that way," says Honey.

"Whoa! I'm sorry I asked," says Greg.

"I must say as pretty as you are, I'm shocked to see that you are single.

"Yes! It's true," says Honey, "it happens to the best of us. I have to be heading on out," says Honey as she goes to her car.

"Could I please see you again?" says Greg.

"Maybe! If you promise to leave room on my caller ID for others. I see your number once, that's all I need to see to know that you called."

"I guess you're right. I cannot be mad at you for making that statement. Could I get a hug?" asks Greg.

"No, I can't do that one," says Honey as she reminisced about her last date.

"Please don't get too close," she says to herself. Greg is not used to being turned down by any woman, and he is the type of man who loves to rush into things.

"Just one hug," asks Greg again.

"Not at this time," yelled Honey! getting agitated with Greg. Greg is the man. So that's what most women think. Women would melt in Greg's arm, but not Honey. Honey finds Greg to be a very handsome guy just so trusty, and this turns her off also. Among other things, because Honey had seen right through Greg. But for some odd reason she really wants to continue to see him. Greg reaches over just a little to get a peck on Honey's lips, and did he get the shock of his life.

"Aaah!" Yells Greg. "What's up?"

"That's what you get," says Honey as she walks to her car and drives away leaving Greg holding his lips. It was around ten o'clock that night when Honey got inside the house and Booby awaits her at the door. Honey calls her mom to see how she's doing.

"Hi, Mom!"

"How was your date tonight?" asks Mary.

"It went okay," says Honey.

"What's wrong? I could hear it in your voice," says Mary.

"This guy, he's good-looking and all and I bet he's the catch of the century, but there is something about him that I just can't seem to catch. But for some reason I'm drawn to him. Where is Dad?" asks Honey.

"He is out getting my prescription at the all-night pharmacy."

While Frank is out getting Mary's prescription, so was Greg at the same pharmacy. Greg purchases some condoms. He thinks he's about to have a sexual encounter with Honey real soon. While Red sits inside of the car waiting for Greg to come out, Frank comes out from the pharmacy and gets inside of the car. Frank drives past Red, and Red notices the car and he read the license number.

Red is very nervous he yells out of the car to tell Greg to put a rush on it. Red jumps from the car and yells to Greg, "I'm gone!" Red jumps into the car and tries to catch up to Frank. "I'm so sorry, brother dear, but I'm on something that's truly deep."

Greg comes out from the pharmacy to see that Red had truly left him. Red drives up behind Frank as he catches up to him to get a glimpse of his face. Red looks at Frank directly in his face, eye to eye. Frank is very unsure as to what is going on right then. As he slows down to see what the guy's problem, Frank then speeds up and drives home with Red driving behind him slowly out of sight. Red has got the address of Frank, and he soon heads toward the pharmacy to pick up his cranky brother.

"This has got to be real good!" says Greg as he yells from the top of his lungs about to have an anxiety attack.

"You remember the time when I told you about the car? I've just seen the car; I followed the car to it's destination and I've got the address. I know for sure his wife had seen my face," says Red.

"But this shit is over with," says Greg. "If they had anything on you, they would have come for you. It could take up to twenty years, and those picnicking cops would still be on the case. There is no such thing as a cold-case file as soon as some idiot comes up with anything," says Red.

"The case is back hot again. I'm not leaving any evidence around," says Red.

"I don't blame you at all," says Greg, "you know how the cops work. They love to linger around."

When Frank arrives home, he tells his wife just what had happened to him.

"It's like the guy was trying to check me out or something. He stared at me in my face watching me and we looked eye to eye. All I want to know is what just happened here," says Frank.

"I really don't know. You just be careful," says Mary.

"I will, dear, I would try my best to," says Frank.

Anthony calls the house to check on his mother to see how she's feeling. Frank picked up the telephone, and he couldn't wait to tell his son the news of what happened to him.

"What! Did you see the make of the car or the license plate?" says Anthony.

"No, son, I really didn't get the license of the car at all. I was not looking for anything of that sort. I really didn't at the time," says Frank.

"Maybe the guy thought that you were someone he had known," says Anthony, "that's why he looked at you and then kept driving."

"No! He slowed down and then he stayed behind me, driving very slow until I couldn't see him anymore. I say something was very fishy," says Frank.

"Just lie down, dear, and don't let it get to you," says Mary.

"Okay, dear, if you say so," says Frank as he dozes off to sleep.

Meanwhile, Honey is at home on the telephone talking to her longtime schoolmate, getting more info about her friend, Eliza.

"You know this is very strange for the two of us to be talking about Eliza's death after almost four long years and fancy running into you again, although we had hardly talked," says Maria.

"Well, you were with your friends; and I was with my one friend," says Honey.

"You know, I spoke with my mother about the murder of Eliza for the first time; I finally asked her a question."

"And what was that?" asks Honey.

"I asked my mother if they ever found out who the guy was or his name or if they had any leads."

"What did she tell you?" asks Honey.

"My mother tells me the guy was a light-skinned Caucasian, and he looked to be a rough neck," says Maria.

"Where does your mother get her information from?" says Honey.

"The lady who used to live next door, but she moved away," says Maria. "I know that the guy's name was Dirtball!" says Maria, "that's what my mother told me."

"Why it took so long for a name to come up?" says Honey. "People need to come forward with information," says Honey. "What if this was a member of their family? How would that person feel? Says Honey.

"You are very concerned!" says Maria.

"I'm very, very concerned," says Honey, "she was a dear friend of mines."

"I would ask my mother some more," says Maria, "if this would help."

"There's nothing I could do. I wish that I could help," says Maria.

"You are sounding like HWAA to me," says Maria.

"And what does that stand for?" asks Honey.

"I'll tell you later," says Maria.

"I think that girl has lost her mind," says Honey as she hangs up the telephone. "I'm not worried about what she says, I'm trying to figure out something," says Honey.

The phone rung just as Honey was about to call her brother. "What's up, sis? Says Anthony.

"You know just when to call," says Honey.

"What do you mean by that?" asks Anthony.

"I just spoke with Maria from school and she was telling me some disturbing news about Eliza's murderer."

"Yeah! What did Maria have to say after three years?" says Anthony.

"There is a name to the bloody face," says Honey.

"Sure!" says Anthony.

"That's what Maria tells me," says Honey.

"So what does this mean?" says Anthony. "Should we go to the police with what we know?" says Anthony.

"I don't know. The police probably know this already," says Honey.

"Why do you say this?" says Anthony.

"The police are very aware of a lot; it's just that they need more proof. You would practically have to be standing right in the police precinct at the time of the crime."

"Meaning standing right there with the knife or gun to the person? Now that's proof enough," says Anthony.

"I miss my friend dearly. I must know who had done this to her. It's like a haunting of some sort, and I just can't shake this feeling off of me. I must do something right away," says Honey.

Anthony says to his sister, "Let us both go to the police just to see how much information they would share with us. We might have some information that they need," says Anthony.

The two arrived to the police station first thing the next morning with plenty of questions. Sitting at his desk was the lieutenant with his foot propped up on his desk.

"How may I help the two of you?" says the lieutenant.

"We're here just to ask you a few questions," says Honey, "if we may."

"Yes! If I could help you out. My name is Glenn, Glenn says as he held out to shake their hand using both of his.

"We are here to ask you about the case on Eliza," says Honey to the lieutenant.

"Oh! I remember that case oh too well," says Glenn.

"Could you tell us anything?" asks Anthony.

"Not much," says Glenn, not much."

"Meaning what!" says Honey. Either you want to or you just can't."

"Well, a little of both. I cannot tell you anything and that I have anything to tell," says Glenn.

"Oh! Now that is just so slow," says Anthony.

"What do you mean?" says Glenn.

"I mean that you tell me all these years, you guys have no clue about the guy who murdered Eliza? I might just know more than you all know up in this place," says Anthony.

"What do you know?" asks Glenn.

"First you tell me something, then I'll tell you something," says Anthony as he sits down. "Do you know the guy's name?"

"Yes, they called him. Red Ball" fire ball, Red bone! Something like that. From what we've heard."

"Oh! Now we're getting somewhere," says Honey.

"So now what?" says Anthony?

"Either the guy has never been in jail before or he's just damn good. I think the guy is still out there. It's just that we don't know how he looks. He may have changed his appearance or something. This guy is one step ahead of us," says Glenn.

"I'll say, he's more than one step away. He's about a good ten step away from you, guys. "You don't know more than we do," says Honey as she tells Anthony to get up.

"Well, don't you two go out trying to be the CIA?" says Glenn.

"Who, me?" says Honey.

"Yes, you," says Glenn. Honey and Anthony walk out from the police station.

"Oh well! That was a trip without the ticket," says Anthony as he gets inside of his car.

"Yes. It truly was," says Honey, "a real bad trip." "I'll catch you later. I'm about to go to the club to work out this body of mines."

"You continue to do that, and you would be nothing but muscles," says Anthony.

While working out, Honey is the center of the attention with the guys. Honey has a body that would knock the booties off of a newborn baby boy as long as his eyes are open. Honey does her work out for the day and starts to head toward home, but she decides to change her mind. She goes to her parents' house instead and sits with the two for an hour. After Honey kisses her parents good-night she leaves and go to her house, she lies on the couch and falls quickly to sleep without making it to her bedroom. The workout must have really tired her out.

Meanwhile Red is up to his old tricks.

"I think it's about that time for us to be heading back to New York," says Greg.

"Not this soon," says Red.

"You were the one who was very bored, why the change all of a sudden?" says Greg.

"Why the change with you? You're the one who was struck by Cupid. Where is the bow and arrow now? Asks Red.

"I'll be back," says Greg, "and when I do, Honey would be my number one whore since she thinks she's too damn good to be my woman."

"You just can't accept rejections, could you? We should have run a train on her," says Red, "before we head back to New York."

"I wouldn't share another thing with you," says Greg, "it's enough I've shared my whores with you."

"So what are we going to do about the guy and his wife before we leave for New York?" Red says.

"For one," says Greg, "you have a new face. I've hardly recognized you myself. How in the hell would anyone remember your dumb ass and it's been three years. I tell you what? I'm not going to worry about it. I'm leaving your dumb ass as soon as tomorrow gets here.

Red sits on the floor looking real dumb while he sits pouting.

"I'm not going anywhere," says Greg to Red. I'm tired and I want to get some sleep. And I'm going to get me some sleep. I suggest that you do the same thing."

The two were quiet for a minute until Red decides to turn on the television. Greg puts the pillow over his entire head so as not to hear a word from Red or the television. On the television, the anchorwoman announces breaking news.

"We have a reason to believe that the murderer of Eliza Ann Finch is still around," says the anchorwoman. "We have more news on the case; the case is officially reopened."

Red starts to get hysterical as he paces the floor. Red takes out his asthma pump; he starts to hyperventilate as he passes out on the floor. Greg is very concerned. Red hasn't done this since he was a young boy. Greg starts to panic not knowing exactly what to do. Greg reaches for his cell phone off the table and starts to call 911. He thought to himself as he hangs up the telephone, I can't do that! I would definitely send him straight to jail instead of the hospital.

Greg rushes into the bathroom to grab a towel off the rack. He then wets the towel and leans over to wipe Red's face, not knowing if this would help any. Red does come to but he was very delirious when he came to. Reaching for his asthma pump, Red discovers he has run out; he starts to wheeze some more. Greg runs through the house shaken up knowing that there is not one spray pump in his mother's house. The two have not been inside of their mother's house in over five years. Red tells Greg to look inside of the car; he has one in the car. Greg runs out to the car and grabs the pump from the glove department and helps his brother out with the pump, and Red begins to get better.

"Don't scare me like that again!" says Greg to his brother. "I don't like that type of bull crap; I get very nervous. We're going to have to keep at least two or three pumps on your ass, man, you gave me a big scare."

The two sit on the couch for a brief minute before they start to pack and leave for New York.

"Before we leave, we're going to stop and get those pumps," says Greg to his brother.

"Man, I might have to go to a side clinic. I don't think I could just go buy one at the store."

"What do you normally do when you run out of your pumps?"

"I go to the clinic up in New York!" says Red.

"Well, we are not in New York now!" says Greg. "Now what are we going to do when you have another attack like the one you just had?

"We are about to leave for New York. I'll stop at the clinic when we arrive to New York. What are we going to do with mom's belongings?" says Red.

"I don't know. I guess we would leave her things the way they are. There is nothing I could do with it," says Greg.

"Call the goodwill or somebody," says Red. "Don't just let her belonging sit here and be thrown out on the street. Someone could use this stuff."

"I guess so. Who we would call?" says Greg.

"Look it up in the telephone directory," says Red, "aren't you the smart one?"

"Don't try and get smart on me!" says Greg.

Red goes inside of his mother's room to look for a telephone book. He finds the telephone book and gives it to Greg.

"Why do I have to look?" says Greg.

"Remember you're the smart one!" says Red. As Greg hangs up the telephone, he tells Red that he would have to leave his mother's key under the carpet at the front door. The goodwill would come out in one week from today's date.

"Oh, we would be long gone," says Red.

"Yeah," says Greg. "I'm not staying another day."

Greg's cell phone starts to ring, and to his surprise it's Honey on the phone. Greg walks away from Red's presence so that he could not be heard.

"I thought that you would never call me again," says Greg, sounding very excited to hear from Honey.

"I'm sorry that I got mad at you for kissing me. I want to apologize and ask you, could I take you out to dinner?" says Honey.

"I would like that very much," says Greg.

"Now this would have to take place tomorrow, if this is okay with you. Now is not the time, besides its kind of late," says Honey.

"I'll be ready tomorrow," says Greg, "I most certainly would." Greg spoke too soon; he hadn't realized this until he walks away into the kitchen to grab a bottle of water from the refrigerator.

Red stood in the door way of the kitchen and says to Greg, "So what do you mean that you will be ready tomorrow." asks Red.

"My! Aren't we very nosy?" says Greg.

"Oh, so forget about me," says Red, "and our whores back in New York?"

"You can go back if you want to," says Greg. "I'm staying another day. I might not ever meet another gorgeous woman like Honey again."

"What about your whores back in New York? Asks Red.

"What about them?" asks Greg?

"You just done gave up on them!" says Red.

"I have not forgotten about my women back in New York. They are the ones who made me what I am today! They know exactly what to do when I'm not around, keep the money flowing. I got it like that," says Greg.

"You just better make sure your whores are still there when you get back to New York. I have spoken with mines, have you?" says Red.

"I don't have to. Didn't I give you two of my whores to get your ass started in the business? If I could give them away to you, then what does that tell you? May I answer my own question? I'm holding it down like that," says Greg as he walks away from out the kitchen leaving Red looking dumb.

"I tell you what," says Greg, "I'm leaving after this date tomorrow, but I would be back to pick up my special package the very next time I'm here in Chicago."

"Damn! This woman has you whipped and she has not even given up the poo nanny," says Red.

"It's not that. I know a real woman when I see one," says Greg.

"What do you think your other women are?" says Red, "Clones of some sort."

"Whores," says Greg, "they are simply whores. I know a woman from a whore. And Honey is my kind of woman. She is headstrong and very smart. She keeps me in suspense, there is a lot to her I want to find out."

Greg would soon find out about the suspense that's driven him so anxiously to Honey's mystery.

Later that next evening, Honey is at home standing in front of her mirror as she admired her body. Honey is very seductive without even trying to be. She has the perfect body any woman would want to have. Honey has a hold on Greg; he's about to be well tamed better than the dog she has at home. As a matter of fact, better than any animal at the zoo. Honey is very unique and witty. She has come to realize that there is more to her charm than meets the eye. Honey wants to know why Greg has secrets, and she intends to find out.

Honey met Greg at the same restaurant as before, and the two are having a nice time until one particular woman walks up to Greg and says to him. "What's up pimping, Greg?"

"What brings you to town?" says Greg.

"Where is that no-good brother of yours?" the young lady asks.

"Do I know you?" asks Greg.

"Oh! So you're trying to be antisocial," the young lady says to Greg.

"No! I'm simply trying to figure out just where I know you from," says Greg as he reaches inside of his pocket to pay the bill, forgetting that Honey was to foot the bill. Honey asks Greg to put his wallet away so that she could pay for their meal. Knowing that she never has to pay for a meal ever, Honey was on to something.

"Oh! You still got it like that," says the young lady.

"You are still taking money from a woman just like that damn good-for-nothing brother. Just the same, no different. You take the woman's money while your good-for-nothing brother takes the poo nanny. I would have called the police, but his weapon was not anything to brag about," she tells Greg.

Greg calls the waiter and hands her a credit card; he drops other cards out from his wallet. Honey sees this and helps him pick up his documents. The young lady storms over to her seat across the way after telling Greg off. Greg excuses himself and tells Honey that he's going to the men's washroom.

"Okay, take your time," says Honey.

Honey starts toward the young lady, but a card on the floor catches her attention. Honey picks up the card, and it appears to have an ID picture of Greg. Honey reads the information.

Why, he lives all the way in New York. I wonder why he's been lying about where he lives. I should have known something, Honey thought to herself. His area code is from another town, which I hadn't thought about until now, she says to herself.

Greg comes from the washroom and sits down to continue his date with Honey.

"I'm so sorry about the incident," he says to Honey.

"So are you saying that you have no idea who she could be," says Honey.

"I have seen her around," says Greg, "but I have no idea who she is."

Honey drops the ID picture of Greg under the table and says to him, "I would like to get some fresh air."

The two got up from the table to walk toward the door, and Honey says to Greg, "Make sure you didn't leave any of your personal belongings on the floor."

"Oh! Yes, let me look around some more" says Greg. Greg finds his picture ID. "I'm so glad you suggested that I look some more. I need this ID. I wouldn't want to pay for another ID when I've just gotten this one."

The two left the restaurant to take a walk in the park which was nearby.

"I'm so sorry about that incident in the restaurant," says Greg.

"Don't be sorry," says Honey, "its okay. I'm not here to judge you at all."

Now Greg loves every minute of this. She's not asking him any question. Honey does have a lot of question deep inside of her head.

"You know, I really don't like being lied to," she says to Greg.

"What do you mean?" asks Greg.

"Are you trying to hide anything?" asks Honey.

"Not really!" says Greg.

Was the young lady a friend of yours asked Honey.

No! Just someone I know says Greg!

"It seems that she has it out for you" say Honey!

"Someone my dear brother knows say Greg!

"I tell you what," says Greg, "could we get on another conversation because I'm" not feeling this conversation say Greg!

"Okay, I think I could do that," says Honey.

Greg leans over to put his arms around Honey. Honey gives Greg a look that made him remove his arm quickly. The two continue to talk some more before they parted. That night Greg thought about Honey. He didn't want to leave for New York, but he had no other choice.

Greg tells Red that he would be back in Chicago as soon as he could. "You better be glad you're my brother," says Greg.

"Oh! Or what you've trade me in for a piece of poo nanny," says Red.

"You've already been traded for some poo nanny. I just have not gotten any just yet," says Greg.

"Damn! You have not taken a shot at that yet," says Red. "She's holding the poo nanny down real good. Now doesn't it make you want to just take the shit, while she's thinking that it's a gold mine of some sort?"

"Really it is her gold mine. She's not using it to get gold but she's storing it because it's her gold, not mines," says Greg.

"I don't get it," says Red.

"You probably never would," says Greg. "I love a woman who makes me wait although I feel rejected, which hurts also. But I also love a woman who holds her own, meaning that she is in full control."

"Why are you pimping then?" says Red.

"Because the women allow me to do this pleasure and there's money involved. If and when I settle down, I would want a woman just like Honey because she holds her own."

"I think that you are off on crack!" says Red.

"No, brother dear, just in love with a strong-minded beautiful woman. Why, if I had my way, I would have my whores to take care of me and Honey. Honey would be the main woman. She would never have to go out and sell her poo nanny; just the whores would definitely be out just like they do for me now. And neither of us would have to work ever again in this life or any other life; why, we would have money for the next life it there's any," says Greg.

"I think you are just as sick as a dope fiend trying to shoot Ajax in his arm."

"No! You're the sick one," says Greg. "Guess who I run into while trying to have a decent date with Honey? Jana! You dumb ass fool, the girl you raped damn there four years ago. I tell you, you are as dumb as dumb could get. You suppose to at least scare the bitch out her wits so that she won't talk at all."

"The next time, I'll kill the bitch to make sure she does not open her mouth ever again. Like I did with the bitch three years ago."

"Now that bitch tried to fuck your ass up. You got a piece of her and she's sure as hell taken out a piece of you," says Greg. "And that was the last time you ever took some poo nanny from anyone, am I'm right or wrong?" asks Greg.

"Well . . . I guess you are right," says Red. Hesitant to respond to his brother.

"How many times have I told you to stop? You would not be in this predicament right now if you had listened to me back then," says Greg. "Everything that looks good is not all that good."

While Red and Greg start packing to leave for New York, the news media flashes right in with breaking news again. With news from three years ago, this time they had an old newscast that was dated from when Mary and Frank spoke about the murder of Eliza. Red watches as he starts to get excited, and Greg holds him tight and tells him to calm down, "we are about to leave from here."

"No! Let's just take care of them right now so that we have no worries," says Red. "At least I wouldn't have this raging over my head wondering if and when these people would bring this shit to court. I don't need to go to jail," says Red. "I know that this woman had seen me. I thought that this shit would be over long ago."

"The shit is never over," says Greg. "It might die down, but it's never over; you said so yourself," said Greg.

"I guess you're right," says Red, "if you don't go with me, I'll go by my damn self."

"Go on with your bad ass," says Greg.

"Oh, so you going to let me go alone," says Red.

"You were born alone," says Greg, "and also you've done the crime alone."

Red storms out of the door went inside the trunk of the car and grabbed something out, start the car, and drives away when Greg runs out from the house fast yelling for Red to slow down.

"I'm sorry, man! But I'm tired of having your back when you do the dumbest shit. You're worse than dumb criminals. They should have a show about you and only you from every dumb thing you've ever done all your life, with your picture on front of the screen. This is my last damn time helping you out," says Greg.

Honey takes a shower, goes toward the couch to sit down, and turns on the television. Booby jumps from the floor onto Honey's lap wanting her attention. The telephone rings, and it's Frank calling to say good night to his Honey girl as he used to call her as a young girl. "How's my Honey girl doing tonight?"

"I'm fine," says Honey.

"I love you, Honey," says Mary as Frank held the telephone to Mary's mouth.

"I love you too," says Honey to her mother.
"Are you on your way to bed?" asks Mary.
"No, not right now," says Honey.
"I just cannot sleep," she says to her mother.
"Try and get you some sleep, dear," says Mary.
"I'll call your brother when we hang up from you," says Frank.
"Was your date okay?" says Mary.
"It went okay. I'm just not going out with the guy anymore. Something about him just won't let me rest," says Honey.
"Hold on a minute," says Frank.
"I think I heard some noise," he tells Honey.
There was some silence for a minute and then Frank went back to talking to Honey.
"What was the noise?" asks Honey.
"I guess it was nothing," says Frank.
Frank heard the noise again, and he tells Honey to hold the line. "It sounds like someone's outside the door."
Who would be at the door this late? There was a knock on the door. Frank froze up for a minute not knowing what to do at that moment. "Are you still there?" asks Honey. "Did you see who it was at the door?"
"I'm afraid to go toward the door," says Frank. Not knowing if the person's has a gun and might shoot through the door says Frank.
"Why is that?" asks Honey. Now Honey is getting a little on the edge to hear her dad act so strange.
"Honey, would you hang up and call Anthony to see If he's home?"
"Why?" says Honey as she starts to get worried? Anthony would call first before coming to the house. "Go see if it's him. I'll hold the phone," says Honey.
"The problem is that there is someone knocking at the bedroom door!" says Frank.
"The bedroom door," says Honey!
The knock comes once more. "Is that you, Anthony?" Frank yells. Mary starts to get very frightened.
A voice from behind the door yells back and says to Frank, "Nope! You dope, that's the wrong answer." Frank is startled now; he has no idea who's at his bedroom door.
"Dad, are you still there," asks Honey.
Frank grabs the telephone and says to Honey, "Who would have the audacity to come into my home and knock on my bedroom door?
"Who is it?" says Honey to Frank. "I don't know, dear, I really can't say."

Greg and Red stood on the outside of Frank's bedroom door and yells at Frank and Mary.

"We said knock, knock," says Red as the two bang on the bedroom door, scaring Mary.

Honey had no choice but to listen to what was going on. Honey yells through the phone and tells her dad that she's on her way.

"No, Honey, don't come, call the police," Frank says to her. Frank has no protection at all, never thought to this day that he would ever need some in his quiet and safe neighborhood.

Honey runs out the door with her cell phone in her hand while still connected to her dad. Honey has no idea who's at her parents' house, but she aims to find out.

Red knocks on the door again even louder as he said the words again, "Knock, knock." Mary starts to scream as Frank held her in his arm to protect her with his comfort. That's was all he had to protect her; he held her tight as he could. Red tells Mary that screaming was the wrong answer.

"The word is who it is?" says Red.

As the two kick the door wide open, Frank jumps away from his wife and yells at Greg and Red. "Get the hell out of my house."

Honey talks through the phone, and no one could hear her at all. The telephone sits right on the bed. Mary tries to reach for the telephone so she could talk to her daughter. Mary reaches for the telephone and tries to say something as she put the phone toward her mouth. Red grabs the phone away from Mary.

"I've been waiting three long years for this day," says Red to Mary. "You hardly recognize me? Do you remember three years ago in the woods? Remember this face for a short minute because you will never be able to tell anyone anything".

Mary thought back to that dreadful night as she tried to cover her face. Red pulls the trigger to the gun and shot Mary between her eyes. Frank hears the gunshot, looks over toward his wife, and sees that she had been shot. Frank knocks Greg down to the floor; he is not going to let these guys go without fighting back. Red comes behind Frank and shoots him in the back of the head.

Greg and Red are brief to the point, leaving very quickly not knowing that Mary was still alive. Honey heard the first shot; she had no idea what it was, but it was loud. Honey had no signal at all. Red puts the telephone on the receiver as the two run out of the house.

Frank lies dead on the bedroom floor. Mary lies across the bed; she moves slowly, trying to cling on with every breath she has, waiting on her daughter, knowing that every second counts, but Mary is not about to give up to death to soon.

Honey arrives to the house after Greg and Red had no sooner left. Honey has no idea who's inside her parents' house. Honey yells out for her mom and dad; there was no answer. Honey yells again and still there was no answer; she dials her brother's number and tells him to come to their parents' house as something has happens to their parents.

Anthony quickly jumps out of bed and heads out the door. With no idea on what was going on, he hears something is wrong and it has to do with his parents; that was all Anthony needs to know.

Honey manages to bring herself inside of her parents' bedroom and what she sees is very disturbing to her. Who? And why would anyone? Honey thinks as she walks over to her parents. Honey couldn't believe her eyes. This has got to be a nightmare.

Frank lies on the floor and Mary lies across the bed. Honey knows right off her dad was dead; she looked over at her mother and sees a sign of life. Honey rushes over to her mother's side. Mary uses her last breath to speak to her daughter for the last time only to speak Eliza's name. Mary died right before her daughter's eyes; Honey could not understand why her mother would mention Eliza's name at the time of her death. Honey closes her mother's eyes, and she lets out a scream you would have thought that another planet heard her cries of death.

Honey walks from her parents' bedroom with a strange look about her; she walks down the stairs. Honey has never had hatred in her heart for anyone. Even when her best friend Eliza got killed. But now this is her own blood shedding, and she feels the pain her parents had to endure. Honey starts to change as she walks down the stairs. She has nothing but pure hatred in her heart, soul, and mind. Honey is changing; her eyes are much darker, and she appears to be getting huge as she grows fuzz about the body. Honey is very grief stricken and is hurting inside. Honey's eyes done enlarge if any larger they may as well pop right out of the socket. Honey has changed; she's no longer all human. She's part human now and part queen bee.

Honey starts to drool at the mouth as her clothes start to rip from her body piece by piece. When Honey reaches the bottom of the stairs, Honey was stark naked, without a string of clothes on, drenching with honey as honey drips from her body. Honey starts to come from Honey's pores as she continues to walk down the stairs. Honey has no sense of direction. She's about to be out of control as she starts to make the buzzing sound, which frightens the neighbors. Some start shutting their windows thinking that there was a swarm of bees nearby. Honey makes the sound again as she opens her mouth. She has eyes between the teeth so that she could see in every direction.

Honey's body is covered now with nothing but fuzz. Honey tilts her head as though to smile but it is a grief-stricken smile. Honey is in great pain, and with what she's feeling, no man would want to touch Honey right about now.

Anthony runs inside of the house; he's shocked to see what he's seeing. He knows that Honey had to be very upset to be in the condition she was, not even he could get her to go into that mode. Anthony watches his sister; he has realized that his parents have to be dead.

Anthony looks at his sister and says before he realizes it, "I would hate to be the one who just upsets you." He went past Honey on the steps.

Anthony went inside of his parents' bedroom, and he sees his parent's dead. He quickly gets on the telephone and calls the police.

I feel like I've just died with my parents, Anthony tells himself. How I would cope now! Anthony goes toward the stairs to see about Honey. Over in the corner toward Honey's old bedroom, Anthony notices something. He walks over toward the object and notices that it is an asthma pump.

"I wonder who this could be," says Anthony, "and what this is doing inside my parents' house." There has got to be a connection." Anthony put the asthma pump inside of his jacket.

Honey has calmed down, and came to her senses as she sits with her hand to her face. Honey looks up as she heard her brother come down the stairs.

"Did you see anything?" asks Anthony.

"No not at all. I know one thing," says Honey, "it was someone outside of the bedroom door. And I believe it to be a male."

"Are you sure?" says Anthony.

"I'm sure," says Honey, "and another thing, right before Mom died, she mentioned Eliza's name to me."

"So do you think Eliza has something to do with this?" says Anthony.

Honey looked at Anthony and says to him now, "How could she come back, and if she could, why would she want to kill our parents?" says Honey.

"Just checking. Everyone and everything around me are strange as ever," says Anthony as he looked at his sister.

"There has been some strange thing going on in this life, I must say." Honey nudges at her brother's side.

"You look a mess. You need to put on some clothes before the police arrive."

"You called the police? Don't say anything at all," says Honey, "about what I've said to you."

"Okay," says Anthony. Honey went upstairs to change from the clothes that were ripped off her body when she had grown enormously.

The police soon arrive with plenty of questions. The neighbors start to come from out of their houses as soon as the police arrive. Hearing the sirens let the neighbors know that they could come out of their houses now, unable to realize if it was still safe to come out. One cop goes door to door while another asks the question. Then more cops arrive on the scene. Honey talks to the police assuring that she has no idea about anything.

"I heard the sound of some bees, which way the bees went, I don't know and I'm not trying to find out," says the lady.

"If you asked me," said one guy, "they were some deadly bees, that's how they sound."

"It was just like death coming," says the old guy, "and these bees where very angry."

"I'm sorry about your parents," says another older lady.

"I've seen the two guys when they jumped into the car and drove off," says the lady.

Honey pulls the lady toward her so that the cop couldn't hear what the lady was saying to her. Honey thanks the older woman for her information and walks over to Anthony. Honey and Anthony try to gather their information.

Anthony's cell phone rings, and it's his wife. He answers the cell phone and tells his wife the bad news. Anna was very upset by the news; it was unexpected to her. She cried on the phone.

"Honey, I'll be home as soon as I can."

"Don't worry about me. You take your time," says Anna.

"I'll see you as soon as I get home," says Anthony.

Honey stands a distance from the house as she quietly cries to herself. Anthony walks over to Honey and says to her, "We have got to find out who has done this, there is no reason for anyone to want to kill our parents."

That night, Honey doesn't stay at her house. She stays the night at Anthony's house. The two go to Honey's house to get her dog and a few items. Anna fixes Anthony and Honey something good to eat. The two aren't in the mood for eating at that moment.

"Do you want to talk? Asks Anna. "Anthony tells me that Mary had spoken your friend's name right before her departure, is that correct?"

"Yes." Honey nudges Anthony again. Anna gets up to get some coffee.

"Didn't I tell you not to say anything to anyone!" says Honey.

"But she's my wife. You know she won't say a word," says Anthony. Anna returns to the table where the three talk while crying for hours at a time.

"Now, what are we going to do about this situation?" says Anna. "Now that we have an idea of what's really going on."

"I know one thing," Honey responds, "I have an idea of who did this to our parents, and I believe that somehow they're also connected to my dear friend Eliza."

"Who are you referring to?" asks Anthony.

"Remember when I told you that mom had mentioned Eliza's name? I believe that she was trying to tell me that the same person who killed Eliza also killed them."

"That might be so. Your mom was very courageous," says Anna.

"I also found this," says Anthony as he pulled out the asthma pump. "This just might belongs to whoever was inside of our parents house last."

Honey's eyes practically lights up with excitement. She smiles at Anthony as she examines the asthma pump to see if it was the same one she had seen Red with the day she had first met the two.

"Greg and Red are the dirty bastards who killed our parents and Eliza. The dream I had was trying to warn me, and so was our mother. We are on a mission, it might just be a slow journey, but it's going to be a quick trip," says Honey.

"The guy I went out on a date with—his brother uses an asthma pump. I heard him call his brother Red maybe its because he's real light, I really didn't care for him," says Honey.

"I wonder why those two target our parents," says Anthony.

"Why would you think that it was those two?" says Anna.

"One reason is because my mother had a bullet to the head. My mother was determined to hold on a little longer. She knew that I was on my way, and with her last breath she had but one word to say," says Honey. "You have known my mother for two years, right? Now you must know that this meant something."

"So it's two guys we're dealing with," says Anthony.

"Yes, it is, and I know exactly who they might be and where they are right now."

"So are you two going to the police with this information?" asks Anna.

"No," says Anthony.

"Why?" asks Anna.

"Honey is the police!" Anthony says to Anna.

"Oh! Is that so," says Anna.

"You haven't seen Honey in action," says Anthony.

Anna has no idea what Honey is capable of when she's uncontrollably excited. But she would soon find out.

"I know the two of you have a plan," says Anna. "Do you know where these guys are? Asks Anna.

"I have an idea," says Honey.

"And where might that be?" asks Anna.

"The two are in New York," says Honey, "if I'm correct."

"New York!" says Anthony very loudly.

"How do you know this?" asks Anna.

"While in the restaurant, Greg dropped his ID, which had all the information I needed, not knowing that it was going to lead to this. I felt something strong about Greg although he's a good-looking man. There were some inconsistencies with his conversation. And not only that, I had a terrible dream about his brother, which made me want to stick around Greg and give him a chance for some odd reason."

"And this was the reason," says Anna.

"I guess some things happen for a reason," says Anthony.

"It's called faith," says Anna.

"All you need is patience," says Honey, "and I guess I must have some because I've been waiting too long for this day to come."

"Now, Ms. Honey, what are you going to do?" says Anthony.

"I'm going to pay the two a visit, that's what I'm going to do. And you're going with me," Honey she tells her brother.

"Without a doubt," says Anthony. "You know I've been waiting for this day to come also."

"What about me?" asks Anna?

"What do you mean?" asks Anthony.

"I want to go to New York with you guys," she says to the both.

"I don't want you to come along, sweetheart, it wouldn't be a pretty sight, believe me," Anthony says to his wife.

The next evening, Anthony and Honey are on their way to New York to pay Greg and Red a visit. While arriving to New York, the two have to walk down the roughest street going in the wrong direction, since the two had never been in New York, not really knowing where to go even with a map.

"What have I told you bitches over and over again? Why do I have to keep on repeating myself?" says the voice nearby.

"That voice sounds very familiar," says Honey to Anthony. The two take a peek around the corner and see Red hollering at two of his whores.

"I see that he's up to his old tricks. We will come back to that one, let's find Greg first. "I really don't know which one of those slick-ass bastards I want to go after first," says Honey.

"Is he one of the brothers?" asks Anthony.

"Yes, that's the one who I believe killed Eliza, and I wonder which one did our parent in," says Honey.

"Well! I know one thing for sure. You don't want any witness. I never thought the day would come when the two of us would not have a kind heart in our soul," says Anthony to his sister.

"I never thought the day would come when our parents would get killed either. I thought you were supposed to live and let live," says Honey to Anthony.

"I know you're right about that," says Anthony. "I'm with you on that quote."

"The world would be a better place if you just live and let live," says Honey again. "But I'll think about that a little later after I do what I come to do."

Anthony says, "You know what, we're on Fourteenth Place when we are suppose to be on Fourteenth Street." The two start to laugh at the street sign above their head. "We have a ways to go." Anthony looks at the map.

Honey flags down a cab and asks the cab to take the two to an address that she remembers on Greg's ID. Once the two had arrive to the address, Honey tells the cab driver to go three blocks down the street, saying to the cab driver, "this is not the right address."

"This is the address you told me to drive to," says the cab driver.

Anthony wonders why Honey would change her mind after arriving at the right address. Honey pays the cab driver and walks ahead of the car. Anthony still tries to figure his sister out. The cab turns the corner and drives away.

Honey turns to Anthony and says to him, "I only wanted to throw the cab driver off. I can't do this knowing that the cab driver would say to anyone that he dropped two persons off at that address."

"Well, I guess you have a point, I think." Anthony says, sounding a little confused. "Good thinking," says Anthony as the two walked three blocks to get to their destination.

The two arrived at Greg's front door. Just as the two arrive at the door, the door opens and out come three of Greg's whores. A cab pulls up and the three get inside as Greg stands in the doorway telling the three to make his money and plenty of it. Greg closes the door while Honey goes to the window and takes a peek inside.

"Is he the guy we're looking for?" asks Anthony.

"Yes, he's the other brother," says Honey to Anthony.

"Now how are we going to get inside of this place?" says Anthony. "Do you think there are others inside the house with him?" asks Anthony.

"I don't know," says Honey, "but we will soon find out."

Anthony walks toward the door and twists the doorknob, and to his surprise the door was not locked.

"His dumb ass forgot to lock the door," says Honey.

"Good," says Anthony, "let's take a peek inside."

The two go inside of the house to get a look, and there is one of Greg's whores sitting at the table.

"I see that she must have time off for good behavior," Honey whispers to Anthony.

The two crept up the stairs without being seen. "We should separate," says Anthony.

"Yes, we should," says Honey as the two went their own separate ways probing through the huge house.

While looking around, Anthony opens the door to one of the bedrooms. To his surprise, some of the whores were still at work while inside. Two of Greg's whores were in business while taking care of one of the johns, the pimps refer to as customers. Anthony quickly closed the door so as not to be seen.

Honey, on the other hand, has been spotted by one of Greg's whores. She comes behind and grabs Honey by the throat. Honey has no idea what is going on, but she assumes she's being attacked by someone from behind. With enough strength, Honey flips the woman, knocking her unconscious with such force on to the floor.

Honey moves the woman away to a corner of the stairs so she could not be noticed. Anthony comes around the corner, and just as Honey walks away, he sees the woman lying on the floor. He says to himself she must have run into Honey.

Anthony steps around the woman as he continues to look for whom he has no idea. Anthony knows that he's going to swing at any male or female that he comes in contact with at anytime while inside this house.

Honey has more strength than she could handle as she crept past the huge statue that stood seven foot tall. Honey says to herself, "Greg got it like that, if I've known this, I would have wiped him out for every cent that he's worth." "I'm just kidding," she tells herself. This man had been doing this line of work for a long time to get where he's at. Meaning that Greg has some expensive merchandise inside of his mansion, not to mention just how much money the mansion must have cost him."

Honey hears someone laughing as she approaches the bedroom ahead. Honey listens at the door.

At this time Anthony walks up, and Honey says to Anthony, "I think he's inside." The two listen at the door. Honey hears Greg's laughter. She assured Anthony that that's his laugh.

"I know that laugh anywhere. I guarantee you this asshole won't ever laugh again," Honey tells her brother.

Anthony knows that Honey's telling the truth. He wouldn't want to be the one Honey's angry with, under no circumstances. Honey asks her brother to hide around the corner. She has one trick up her sleeve.

"I'll be your bodyguard," says Anthony.

"You don't have to worry about ever guarding this body." Honey puts her hand on her body.

"I'm quite aware of that," says Anthony. "I guess I'll just stand outside the door, while you handle your business.

Honey knocks at the door of the bedroom. Anthony looks around the corner at his sister and asks her, "Why are you knocking at the door?"

Anthony kicks his leg out toward Honey motioning her to kick the door in. Honey stands at the door knocking. Anthony whispers to Honey, "Are you off just a little bit?"

The voice of a woman asked who it is.

"It's me, Honey!"

"What is the matter with you," Anthony whispers to Honey. "Just kick the damn door in." Anthony now has the jitters as he is trying to get Honey's attention.

The two have come too far for Honey to start getting curdiest toward the enemy. Just as Anthony walks toward Honey to ask her what was the matter, the door opens. Anthony hide away so as not to be seen. Honey knows exactly what she is doing, although Anthony thinks his sister has lost her mind.

Honey was greeted by an older woman who looked to be around her own mother's age.

"Who's at my bedroom door?" says Greg, "this has got to be damn good."

No one was aloud to knock on Greg's bedroom door when he's teaching his women more tricks about the trade. Greg lies back while he's in bed with four of his whores handling his business sexually.

"I haven't done my business just yet," he yelled out, "this has better be damn good."

Honey walks inside of the room. Greg's eyes are as big as his groins right about now. Greg truly was glad to see Honey but not under these circumstances.

"What are you doing here in New York? Who let you inside," says Greg, "without my permission?" Greg has so many questions knowing that he's busted for who he really is. But that's not the reason, although Honey doesn't care what kind of life Greg leads.

"I can explain," says Greg.

"You do not have to explain anything to me. I'm not your woman," Honey says to Greg.

"I just come to see how you are doing. I was in the neighborhood."

"Oh! You just happen to be in my neighborhood all the way in Chicago," says Greg.

"I have an aunt who lives out here," Honey tells Greg.

"Yeah!" says Greg as he proceeds to get dressed.

"How did you know my address?" asks Greg.

"You don't have to get dressed," Honey says to Greg.

"Why not?" Greg asks.

"I want to get in your bed with you," Honey says to Greg.

"Now you're talking," Greg says to Honey.

Honey bumps one of the ladies and tells her to move over. "There's a new poo nanny in town. I'm quite sure Greg wants some new poo nanny."

"I sure as hell do," Greg says as he grins at Honey with all of his teeth.

One of Greg's women is a little upset as she walks toward the door to go out. "You could just march your ass right back over here," Greg say to his whore.

Greg starts to nibble on Honey's ear. Honey starts to buzz. Just the slightest touch from Greg angers her. Honey grabs hold of Greg's face as though she's about to kiss him. Honey has a death grip on Greg's face as she takes one hand toward Greg's neck and grips him tight.

Greg says to Honey, "You are very feisty and controlling. I like that in a woman."

As Greg leans to kiss her, Honey smiles at Greg while she says to him, "I have a story to tell since I have your attention."

Honey held on to Greg's neck very tightly. "Not so tight," says Greg to Honey as he starts to squirm.

"What is your story?" Greg asks Honey.

Honey leans over toward Greg's ear and whispers to him softly, "Remember the two people you killed in Chicago?" Greg tries to pull away from Honey's tight grip. Greg couldn't believe what he was hearing from

Honey's mouth. How could Honey have known about that? Greg asks himself.

"Those two people you killed where my parents," she tells Greg as she stood over him.

Honey looks into Greg's eyes as her eyes twirls around in circles. Honey starts to make the buzzing noise that she makes when she's about to go into her change of appearance.

Anthony covers his ears; the buzz sound was so excruciating. It was annoying and nerve destructing to anyone's ear. Honey's appearance quickly changes as she stands having a tight grip on Greg's head. Honey's clothes start to bust as she becomes intensively angry while she speaks to Greg about her parents.

"Why! Why would you kill two lovable people that meant so much to me out of anything in the world?" Honey now stands stark naked in front of Greg. Although this is what Greg wanted, now is not the time. Honey stands in the flesh as she had come into the world looking so seductive, aiming to do something very destructive.

Honey says to Greg, "This is where you get off at if you really want to get off. Watch this sexy gorgeous body." She stands up in the bed still gripping Greg's throat.

"Do you see this body? You could have had all of this," Honey says to Greg looking Greg right into his eyes; she begins to sweat honey from within as the honey slowly leaks throughout Honey's body.

Greg watches Honey's sexy body as honey slowly eases out from Honey's pores onto her voluptuous body. I don't think Greg wants a taste of Honey. Not right now. Greg tries to plead with Honey, realizing that now isn't the time to beg.

"Help me, you whores, there are four of you. Don't just stand there. Kick her ass."

Honey stood naked, but she wasn't hesitant to fight with the quickness. Honey makes sound as if bees are surrounding her. Honey's body begins to take its course as she manifests right before Greg's eyes. One woman charges at Honey, but Honey back-swipes her with the back of her fist, knocking the woman into the wall.

Anthony opens the door to take a peek inside to see if Honey is okay. Honey kicks the door shut very quickly.

"Fine time for her to kick now," Anthony says to himself.

"Please, I'm sorry, I had no idea that they were your parents," says Greg to Honey. "My brother, he did the murder, it was not me."

"You're just as guilty, you could have stopped him," says Honey with a trusty sound from deep inside of her voice.

"My brother says that they knew about the murder three years ago and that he wanted to shut up the lady from talking."

"Eliza was my best friend; now that's double trouble for you," she cries out loud.

"Get this wild woman right now," says Greg as his voice weakens with Honey's tight grip. Honey rips Greg's head off as she makes a deviating sound which makes everyone hold on to their ears. Honey stands on the bed with Greg's head in her hand as she climbs out from the bed to walk out the door.

Just as Honey turns to go toward the door, one woman tried to run out the door. Honey quickly knocks the woman down to the floor with Greg's head as she plays the slugger in the outfield. Honey now has fuzz all around her body. Honey slams Greg's head into the door as she swung at another woman trying to get out the door. Greg's head goes through the door. Anthony looks over his head and jumped about ten inches from the floor being scared out of his wits seeing Greg's head.

"What the hell!" says Anthony out loud before he had realizes what he said. Honey has no choice but to do what she set out to do if it meant killing everyone who got in her way. Honey beats the four whores to death with what was left of Greg's head. Honey walks down the stairs with Anthony right behind her. Honey walks down the stairs still holding on to Greg's head.

"Why are you still holding on to the head?" says Anthony.

"This is my weapon, do you mind?" says Honey as she comes to herself.

Anthony turns his head to keep from looking at his sister's nakedness. "I know damn well you're not going outside like that. We have got to find you some clothes while you're going around busting out of every outfit that you own. Do something about that head. I'm not going to be walking down the street with you while you are carrying that thing," says Anthony. "Let us find some clothes for you to wear on the street before we leave out of this house. The man has great taste said Anthony. The two searches the house and find Honey some clothes that belonged to the women.

"Good taste in clothes," says Honey to Anthony as she tries on the clothes. "Very expensive also."

"I shall say Anthony" says to Honey as she walks out the door.

Maybe I've should have had me some Hooker" Whores on my arms!

"You better quit playing with me." She looks at her brother and laughs, finding her brother to be amusing. "Oh wait! I forgot something," she tells Anthony.

"Where are you going?" asks Anthony. Honey runs back into the house and up the stairs toward the bedroom where Greg's body is.

Returns with a brown bag.

"Honey stood wearing a unique expensive short mini skirt looking more like a call—girl blended in as a hooker-whore with her stiletto high heels on." Anthony stands in the doorway laughing.

"We have one more case," says Honey to Anthony. "Let me handle this one."

"You just handle one," Anthony says to his sister.

"Yes, and I'm going to handle this one also so that it would be fast and very discreet. We have to get back to our side of town," Honey tells Anthony, "And before someone discovers the mess I've made back there at the mansion."

"I'm on your side all the way," says Anthony to Honey, "let's do this."

The two find Red where they had last seen him although; this time he is beating the crap out one of his whores. The woman runs into a corner to hide from Red.

"There is nowhere for you to hide," he says to the woman, "I've got your ass cornered."

"I guess this is right up your alley; do what you do best," Honey says to Red as she walks his way. The woman tries to run away. Red grabs her by the throat and pushes her up against the wall.

"What are you doing here?" asks Red.

"I'm tending to some important business," she says to Red.

"Well! So am I, can you leave for a minute while I tame my whore?"

"I don't think I'm ready to leave too soon," says Honey.

"If I have to say it again, I'm going to have to forget how much my brother cares for you."

Anthony stands far away when he heard Red spoke to Honey that way. Honey grabs Red around his neck and tells the woman to run away. Red tries to swing and hit Honey while she holds his neck literally in the palm of her hand.

"What are you doing? You have a tight grip there," says Red to Honey. "Could we just talk about this? If it's the women, I'll change; just let go of my neck."

Honey has Red with only one hand around his neck; that's how much strength she has to her when she's highly angry. "You love to beat up women. You are a measly little wussy. You love to take what does not belong to you. Also you took my parents' life," she tells Red, "and my best friend's life also. Do you have any idea what you have done to my life over the past three years and now? Do you? Answer me!"

"I'm trying to if you would let go of my neck." Red wiggles himself loose as he drops to the ground running to a near—by corner.

Don't run and hide now you little wussy!

"You killed my parents," says Honey.

"I'm sorry," says Red.

"Don't be sorry now," says Honey to Red. "You can save the sorries. I've heard enough of stories. With your sorry looking ass. Look what I've got." She pulls out something from behind her back that was in a brown paper bag. She drops it on the ground. Anthony walks toward his sister to get a look at what Honey dropped on the ground.

"Well, what have we here," says Honey to Red. "Oops, it's your brother's penis. You know what I'm going to do since you like taking poo nanny from the women. I'm going to do to you the same thing I've done to your brother so that you will never take poo nanny again from women."

Red tries to run from Honey, but Anthony blocks his way. "Let me do this first," she says to Red. "Open your mouth real wide for me, okay?" she tells Red.

"No! Get that away from me," Red says to Honey.

Honey grabs the bag, picks the penis off the ground, and sticks it into Red's mouth. She held Red's mouth shut very tight with the strength that she has. Honey takes Red's head and makes his mouth move very slowly while making him chew down on his brother's penis. You could see Greg's penis drooling from Red's mouth.

"Are you full?" she tells Red. "No, you have not had enough. Look, I'm going to do you a favor before I kill you."

Red looks at Honey and says to her, "You are a crazy-ass bitch. I told Greg you were crazy."

"Yes! And this crazy-ass bitch is going to kill you just like you did my parents."

Red now starts to throw up all over Honey's shoes.

Oh! Now you dumb" dummy now look what you've done!

Honey grabs Red's crouch and clung to it telling Red that he's going to take his clothes off or she's going to snatch his penis from his pants, "You would not have any use for this anymore."

Red starts to stutter while shakening in his shoes.

Red slowly takes off one shoe and than another.

You are moving too dam slow for me Honey said.

Honey whisper to Red in his ear" do you want me to take it all off piece by piece.

Because if I have to do it you wouldn't like it.

Red starts to move just a little bit faster!

But not fast enough for Honey.

Honey shocked Red right were his favor for the pleasure was.

Red starts to drop his clothes faster by the moment at this point.

That's the way I like it says Honey while she whispers into Reds ear.

Honey grabs hold to her mouth and say to Red is this the weapon you use on these women that you took poo—nanny from.

You should be lock up for this little thing.

Honey shook her head you need your ass kick and I'm the one who's going to kick your ass.

Honey quickly turns into the queen of all bees as she is surrounded by a swarm of bees. Anthony runs and hides as the colony of bees demolishes Red and all you heard is Red screaming like a little wussy. As the colony of bees attacks and eats through Red's flesh.

Anthony walks toward the way to see what happened. Honey comes from the court way of the alley. "What happened?" says Anthony.

"I don't think you want to know," says Honey. Anthony, being nosy, had to take a look any way. Anthony sees Red skeleton, and over on his side was his penis. This is too disgusting for even the bees to touch. I guess Red got a taste of honey whether he wanted or not.

INDEX

A

accident 39
  play with bees 10
  Mrs. Rogers 50
Anthony. *See* William, Anthony
attacker. *See* criminals

B

bees 10, 14, 15, 38, 46, 56, 76
  beehive 10
  queen bee 28, 74
  swarm of bees 75, 87
breakdown 37

C

Caucasian 62
Chicago 9
  murder 51
  neighborhood 39, 73
clutches 30
conversation 35
cover up 42
  makeup 42, 43
  surgery 50
crime scene 35, 38
  woman's apartment 43
  woods 34, 36
criminals 40
  man with blood 35

D

date 25
  at the park 27
  at the same restaurant 68
Dirty Red. *See* Rogers, Red
doctor 50, 53
  observation 15
  psychiatrist 10
dream 28, 40, 56, 77

E

electric shock 14, 38
evidence 35, 61
  asthma pump 51, 75, 77
  fingerprints 44
  scars 40, 42

F

Finch, Eliza 21, 31, 34
  dead body 35, 36
  fingers 35, 49
  friend 22
  funeral 42, 43, 44
  murder 37, 62
forest 9, 13
Frank. *See* William, Frank
funeral commotion 45
funeral coordinator 44

G

Greg. *See* Rogers, Greg
gunshot 73

H

Honey. *See* William, Honey
   secret ordeal 19
hospital 10, 15, 32, 50, 53

I

information 40
   ID picture 69
   plate number 43, 61
   questions 76
   telephone number 54
insect 31
   wings 22

J

Jim 22, 23, 25, 26, 27, 32, 33

L

leads 62
   description 40

M

Maria 58, 62
marks 10, 21, 49
Mary. *See* William, Mary
Mrs. Finch 36, 44
   death 46
murder 58
murderer. *See* criminals

N

nectarines 11, 26
newborn baby 15
   eyes 16, 17
   tantrums 17

news 71
   another murder 47
   case reopened 65
   Eliza's murderer 63
   of Frank 61
   of Honey's parents 76
   on Mrs. Rogers condition 53
New York 41
   address 69, 79
   arrival 78
   corner 79, 85
   departure 50
   lifestyle 49
   transactions 58
nightmares 10

O

ordeal 15, 48

P

pharmacy 60
poo nanny 41, 82
power 28, 46
   buzzing 16, 17, 28, 37, 74, 83
   death grip 82
   speed 20
   touch 19, 25
pregnancy 10, 16
   contraction 12, 14
prey 30
   meat 30
puberty 19, 47

R

Red. *See* Rogers, Red
Rogers, Greg 49, 50, 52, 61, 65
   death 84
   grief 53
   line of work 58
   mansion 80
   on Honey 51, 59, 69

physical characteristics 52
pimping 41
shock of his life 60
telephone calls 55
Rogers, Red 35, 40, 49, 65
  behavior 42
  death 87
  scars 43

S

secretion 83. *See* trance
sensation 27, 28, 82
slumber party 32
sound of bees 11, 14, 21, 37, 76
sticky stuff 32, 39
Sunday 9, 49

T

track team 19
  Coach Bob 20
  Gerald 20
trance 11, 15, 27, 28
  blackness 27
  eyes 37
  furry hair 37

W

whores 41, 49, 79, 80, 83, 84
William, Anthony 9
  imagination 12
  incident 12
  light stinging 38
William, Frank 9
  death 73
  proposal 9
  work 11
William, Honey
  birth 17
  eyes 74, 75
  grip 27
  Honey girl 17
  runner 19

William, Mary 9
  death 74
  memories 9
  strength 15
  sweet tooth 10
women 41, 42, 60, 67, 70, 81